Scandalized
by a Scoundrel

An All's Fair in Love Novella

By Erin Knightley

Scandalized by a Scoundrel

Copyright © 2013 by Erin Knightley

ISBN: 1493681745
ISBN-13: 978-1493681747

Dedication

To John Moock, who read my short story in our high school English class and jokingly told me it was only a few hundred pages short of being a great novel. It's the little things that plant the seeds sometimes.
Also to Nicole C, who never doubted I'd be on the shelves someday. Thanks for all the encouragement along the way!

And for Kirk, although I'm fairly certain I was the one who scandalized you when we first met.

Books By Erin Knightley:

The SEALED WITH A KISS Series
More Than a Stranger
A Taste for Scandal
Flirting with Fortune
Miss Mistletoe – A Penguin eSpecial

The PRELUDE TO A KISS Series
The Baron Next Door (June 2014)

The ALL'S FAIR IN LOVE Series (Novellas)
Ruined by a Rake
Scandalized by a Scoundrel

Chapter One

*F*or a man with a pistol pointed at his chest, the trespasser seemed rather disconcertingly unconcerned.

Amelia Watson adjusted her grip on her weapon and repeated her question. "What business have you on my father's lands, sir?" She didn't waver at all, instead holding steady and true on her target. Her exceptionally *broad* target. The man's chest was nearly as wide as his patronizing smile.

"If these lands are your father's, then clearly I have taken a wrong turn." He tilted his head, his dark gaze raking over her from the lacy bottom of her dainty pink morning gown to the top of her beribboned straw bonnet before landing again on the pistol in her outstretched hand. "I must say, you make for a very unique welcoming committee for poor, lost souls who have unwittingly wandered across property lines."

What kind of accent was that, anyway? Yes, he spoke the King's English, but there was a flavor to it that she didn't quite recognize. Not Scottish or Irish, but definitely something. His looks gave no hint to what it might be. His eyes were nearly the same color as his hair, both dark and shining in the morning sun. Based on his tanned skin, she'd wager he spent quite a bit of time in the elements.

His light gray wool jacket fit well enough but certainly wasn't of the best quality. Nor were his boots, which were clean and polished but obviously well-worn. Stubble shadowed his cheeks, as though he'd gone a day or two without the benefit of a razor. Even so, his eyes seemed intelligent, his posture proud. He didn't *look* like a man who was looking for trouble, but she couldn't be sure.

And really, what did a villain look like? According to Papa, half the members of parliament were criminals.

Grateful for the solid weight of the pistol's brass grip, she lifted her chin. "There are poor, lost souls, and there are those up to no good. Speak now as to your purpose here before I make up my own mind and act accordingly."

She was careful to control her breathing, not giving away the fact that her heart was pounding like a runaway horse. It had been since the moment he appeared from the copse of trees lining her favorite path. Perhaps she should have listened to Papa's warning not to go walking unaccompanied. Although, to be fair, he had issued the same warning, for as long as she could remember, every time she stepped foot outside the house.

The man lifted an eyebrow, everything about him showing a complete lack of worry regarding her and her flintlock. "You are aware there is a wedding this week on your neighbor's estate?"

Heat that had nothing to do with the late-summer sun stole up her cheeks. Of course…the wedding. Eleanor had invited her weeks ago, but Amelia hadn't even thought about the fact that guests were sure to be arriving early.

Although… She narrowed her eyes speculatively at the handsome intruder. Most everyone in the area knew about the coming nuptials, so it was possible he was merely using the event as an excuse. "I am indeed aware—as is nearly everyone else in a twenty-five-mile radius. Do you have some sort of proof that you are a guest?"

One corner of his mouth quirked up. "Of course. Here, let me just fish my engraved invitation from my coat pocket, where I keep it for just such an occasion as this." He made no move toward his jacket, not that she expected it. He was clearly mocking her.

She glared at him, unamused. "Fine, then be off with you. Do not return, sir, or you will find me somewhat less hospitable."

His brows lifted halfway up his forehead. "*Less* hospitable? Shall I be drawn and quartered then?"

The gun grew increasingly heavy in her hand, but she refused to back down. She didn't know this man from Adam, and his flippant attitude put her on edge. "If you're lucky."

He chuckled softly and tipped his hat. "Very well. I can take a hint. Good day, Miss Watson."

Her eyes widened at the mention of her name. "Wait," she exclaimed, stopping him mid-turn. Dropping the gun to her side, she peered at him with renewed interest. "How did you know my name?"

One single brow lifted as he tilted his head. "I don't imagine there are many pistol-wielding, beautiful young women in these parts." He tapped his forehead. "Deductive reasoning."

With that, he turned and walked away, leaving her hot-cheeked and stunned. A moment later, a slow, reluctant smile came to her lips. Apparently her reputation preceded her. She stuffed the pistol back into the deep pocket at her hip where she always carried it and set off for the house.

It would seem a visit to her neighbor's estate had just been added to her agenda.

***

"You said she was a pistol, but I don't recall the warning that she'd be *carrying* one." Gabriel Winters cocked an eyebrow in his friend's direction as he joined the man in the modest billiards room occupying the northeastern corner of the manor house's second floor. Neither one of them were much for billiards, but it was a quiet room where they wouldn't be bothered.

Setting down his freshly polished foil, Nicolas Norton chuckled. "Does it matter? I should think you'd be used to looking down the barrel of a gun by now."

"Yes, of course. It was the person holding the gun that gave me pause." As a soldier, Gabriel was more acquainted with the business end of weapons than most, but this encounter was certainly a first.

"Why was that?" Norton asked, stuffing his cleaning supplies back into a small leather satchel. There were servants who could do such jobs, but for as long as Gabriel had known him, Norton had preferred to tend to his own weapons, both for war and sport.

Gabriel rolled his eyes. "You're getting married, man, not going blind. If you've laid eyes on the girl, you know full well she's a dark-haired Botticelli's Venus in the flesh." There was no denying her beauty, even if she was a bit of a shrew.

Nick snorted. "I certainly hope there were more clothes involved than that."

"Unfortunately, yes." Though she had stopped him dead in his tracks even clothed —a reaction that had nothing to do with the sudden appearance of the flintlock. "I'm just glad your betrothed told me about the other guests who would be attending the wedding breakfast. She wasn't kidding, either—the girl is fit for Bedlam."

It hadn't been hard to figure out who she was— how many young women of quality would be within walking distance of this place, after all—and it was worth taking the guess just to have seen the absolute shock on her face.

He'd enjoyed catching her off guard. She'd been unreasonably highhanded with him. Not unexpected from an Englishwoman of her class, especially after she'd heard his accent. In his experience, the females of the beau monde were always eager to look down their noses at someone like him.

"Eleanor said no such thing. She simply said Miss Watson is a tad unorthodox."

It was Gabriel's turn to snort. "A tad unorthodox? That's like saying old King George is simply having a bad day." The girl was downright peculiar. Beautiful, but peculiar.

His friend raised an eyebrow. "Watch it there, Winters. He may be mad, but he's still our king."

"Yours, maybe. I'm only half tied to the man."

"And yet you risked your life on the battlefield for him. Now who's peculiar?"

Yes, there was that. "I risked my life for the fame and fortune, of course," he said, holding a straight face. "Ole Georgie never entered into the equation."

Nick threw him an unconvinced look. Tilting his head, he said, "Come to think of it... Didn't you choose the British militia because the Yanks wouldn't have you?"

He was right, damn the man. It still rankled that they had turned him down because of his English citizenship. It wasn't his fault his mother chose a bloody Englishman for her husband. As soon as his father died, Gabriel had happily accompanied his mother back to New York. He may not have been born an American, but it was sure as hell in his blood. "Something like that."

Nick snapped his fingers, his eyes going wide. "Christ, I keep forgetting. This is all moot now anyway. With your new title, you're more English than I am."

Gabriel blinked, his mind readjusting to his new future all over again. And here his father had thought it safe to marry a rich but inferior—in *his* eyes—American since he already had an heir and a spare from his first wife, an English paragon if there ever was one.

Too bad he hadn't counted on his eldest sons' sins coming back to bite him in the arse. With one brother dead from a duel with a cuckolded husband and the other recently buried following a drunken fall from his horse, the title now came to Gabriel, the unwanted mongrel third son. Taking a deep breath, he pushed away the unpalatable thoughts of his new and unwanted station. "Never say it, my friend. Now back to this neighbor of yours."

A rustle at the door had them both turning their heads. Miss Abbington, Norton's lovely step-cousin and soon-to-be wife, leaned into the room. "What's this I hear about our neighbor?"

Norton tsked, folding his arms over his chest. "Eavesdropping, are we?" A foolish grin lit his face at the very sight of the woman. Damn, but the man had turned into a sap. And apparently so had Gabriel, since the sight of Norton's love-struck face made him smile. Somehow, the man had managed to find the very best this country had to offer, and Gabriel was honestly happy for him.

Not that he was in any way envious. He had a plan, and it sure as hell didn't involve any English woman.

"No, I wasn't eavesdropping," she replied, rolling her eyes. "I was looking for you to remind you that the vicar would be here within the hour. And I wished to ensure that you had recovered from your rather sound defeat this morning."

"I beg your pardon," Norton said, mock affront lacing his words. "That wasn't defeat; that was *surrender*."

Something about his response made her cheeks flare pink, and Gabriel decided to intervene before he learned more than he wanted to know about their fencing

7

match this morning. Clearing his throat, he said, "So, yes—I made Miss Watson's acquaintance this morning. Or rather, I made the acquaintance of her pistol. *Lovely* girl."

His interruption did the trick. Miss Abbington's eyes snapped to his as her hand flew to her mouth. "Oh dear. You must have wandered onto Sir Elroy's property. Well, at least she didn't shoot you. I imagine that means she likes you." She smiled broadly, almost encouragingly.

His brow lifted in disbelief seconds before he laughed out loud. "Yes, how very hospitable of her. She is aware that we are not in the middle of some untamed wilderness, yes?"

Miss Abbington came fully into the room and settled beside her betrothed on the sturdy, masculine sofa. Norton's hand casually curled around her shoulders, as though Gabriel weren't sitting right there in front of them. Sighing, she said, "You mustn't blame her. Her father is a bit... Well, it's not my place to speak of their business, but suffice it to say she has good reason for being cautious around strangers."

"My, that makes me feel *so* much better," he said, light sarcasm frosting his words. "Should I be concerned she'll be armed at the wedding breakfast? Perhaps armor is in order?"

She chuckled, amusement touching her dark eyes. "What, are you afraid of a little ole female?"

"Of course I am. I'm afraid of all females."

"Smart man," Norton said, earning a smack on the shoulder. "What?" he asked, the word couched in laughter. "A smart man knows he's no match for a woman. Especially a woman bearing a weapon."

She gave him a tart, knowing smile. "Ah—so you did learn something from our match this morning."

"Indeed," he said solemnly, nodding. "I learned that a woman's kisses following a win are so much more enthusiastic than the ones doled out after a defeat."

Gabriel swallowed a laugh, wondering if that was his cue to leave the two lovebirds. Before he could do anything, though, she came to her feet. "In that case, I shall make doubly certain not to lose to you in future matches." Her eyes sparkled with mischief as she winked and headed for the door. "Now, don't forget to be ready within the hour. Lord Winters, do enjoy your day."

They both watched her as she left, her shiny black braid swinging with each step. "You know, Winters," Norton said at last, smacking his hands on his knees and offering a rueful smile. "In my experience, a woman who knows her way around a weapon is the very best kind."

Gabriel gave a snort of laughter. "I think I'll take your word for it on that one."

***

"Amelia Lynnette Watson, where have you been?"

Drat. Squeezing her eyes closed for a brief moment, Amelia drew a deep breath before backing up a few steps to the doorway of the library. "Good morning, Papa. I was enjoying a walk in this fine weather. How are you?"

Folding his paper and dropping it into his lap, he glowered at her from his favorite reading chair. His perpetually downturned mouth sagged even further than usual, not unlike warmed candlewax succumbing to gravity. "How am I? Perhaps you should have asked yourself such a question before deciding to linger so long during your walk, young lady. You know very well how much strain that puts on my nerves, especially since you insist on going alone."

Young lady? Papa must be more piqued than usual. At five-and-twenty, it had been a while since she had heard that particular moniker. Conjuring her most contrite smile, Amelia said, "My apologies, Papa. Shall I ring for some tea to settle your nerves?"

Exhaling gustily, he nodded. "I suppose so."

Suppressing a sigh of her own, Amelia strode to the bellpull and summoned the maid. Tea fixed just about anything in their household. She knew from experience that apologies followed by tea were the best antidote to her father's censure. "What news from London?"

It was the perfect distraction, as she well knew. His brow lifted as his pale fingers caressed the copy of *The Times* sitting in his lap. "Dreadful. So terribly dreadful." He shook his head sadly, but Amelia could see the gleam in his pale blue eyes. The backward slide of the modern world was his very favorite subject. "The things going on in our capital are enough to make one shiver."

Settling onto the sofa across from him, she let him go on about the various bills, laws, and crimes dominating the paper. There was no use asking him about the positive stories or the society pages; he never bothered to read them. No matter, though—she always read the paper for herself when he was done. It was amazing how different the world seemed when she looked at it through her own filter.

When the tea came, she went about pouring them each a cup: undoctored for her father, a splash of milk for her. "I thought perhaps I would call on Eleanor and Lady Margaret today. The wedding is coming up, and it'd be fun to talk over all the details."

Details such as who Amelia's uninvited guest was this morning. She could hardly wait to speak to Eleanor. With the excitement of the whirlwind betrothal at the house party at her uncle's estate last month, Amelia had hardly seen her since her return.

"Mmm," he hedged, taking a sip of his tea. "Are you sure that's a good idea? You've already been out half the morning."

She sighed and took a bite of the lavender scone Cook had sent up with the tea. Chewing slowly, Amelia savored the soothing blend of herb and honey. She'd learned over the years that her father was more likely to be persuaded if she took a few minutes to act as though she was carefully considering his thoughts.

Swallowing, she said, "True, but I think it would be a lovely way to share in our neighbor's joy. As you know, half of the family won't be coming." It was such a wonderful occasion, she hated that anyone would take it for granted. To her, weddings in the case of a love match were the happiest of all occasions. With her unique circumstances, Amelia had long ago accepted that she would never be able to have the husband and family she had dreamed of as a child, so watching those she cared for find such joy was always a reason to celebrate.

She leaned forward, meeting her father's gaze. "I believe I'll take the carriage, as I wouldn't wish to overexert myself. Do you think Falks would mind escorting me?"

Setting down his cup, Papa shook his head. "No, of course not. Very good of you to think of him."

She smiled serenely and sipped her tea. Requesting Falks was the surest way to set her father's mind at ease. At over six feet tall, their head groom was an intimidating presence, especially with his crooked nose and scarred cheek. He was also as kind a man as she had ever known, able to instantly calm horses and humans alike with little more than a handful of quiet words. It was a talent for which Amelia was very grateful, especially on those days when Papa was particularly anxious.

Those days seemed less and less frequent, thankfully. Still, she would have to be careful not to do anything to upset him again as she had this morning.

Her thoughts drifted back to the man she'd met on her walk. He was every bit as tall as Falks but with an entirely different presence. Flippant, fearless, insouciant—nothing about him said kindness or patience. He seemed like the sort of man who owned whatever space he was in. Including *her* property, apparently.

She took another bite of her scone, picturing the way his gaze had boldly traveled up and down her body. Clearly not a true gentleman. She swallowed, taking a quick drink to combat her suddenly dry throat. Even though Amelia knew she should leave well enough alone when it came to the man, her curiosity overrode her good

12

sense. Eleanor would surely be able to fill in the blanks where he was concerned. The very moment it was late enough to pay a call on her friend, Amelia planned to do exactly that.

Chapter Two

"*A*melia! How wonderful to see you." Eleanor grinned broadly and motioned for Amelia to come join her in the small conservatory.

"And you," she replied, pausing to nod her thanks to the butler before stepping down into the miniature paradise. She wended her way through potted plants and around a bubbling fountain to where her friend stood beside a decorative rack full of exotic-looking flowering plants, watering can in hand. "It's so lovely here," Amelia said, pausing to draw in a lungful of the earthy, humid air. "I could easily lose myself in a place like this."

"Better you than me," Eleanor said ruefully, setting the can down and brushing off her hands. "But it does help to pass the time when all I can do is wish for the wedding to hurry up and get here." She leaned forward conspiratorially. "Especially when my betrothed is off gallivanting with someone other than me."

Amelia laughed at Eleanor's sarcastic eye roll.

14

"The scurrilous swine—what is he thinking, leaving you behind like that?"

A gust of wind blew in through the open windows, rustling the palm fronds and sending loose leaves fluttering across the tiled floor. Eleanor brushed a few errant strands of hair from her eyes and chuckled. "I have no idea. I suppose he thinks that just because he has a friend in town, he should spend time with the man. And speaking of Lord Winters," she said, raising her eyebrows with a mischievous grin, "I've heard you've met."

Lord Winters? Amelia only just managed to keep her jaw from dropping open. The man was a nobleman? But what of his strange accent? And the very ungentlemanly manners? And his lack of alarm at having a weapon pointed at him? She had so many questions; she didn't even know where to start. Pressing her lips together, she nodded in acknowledgment of Eleanor's statement. She wasn't sure she wanted to know what *Lord* Winters had said about the encounter. After all, holding a wedding guest at gunpoint wasn't the most neighborly thing she'd ever done.

Eleanor broke out in a wide smile. "It sounded as though you made quite an impression."

The unexpected heat of a blush crept up Amelia's neck. What her friend must think of her. "I'm *so* sorry about— "

"No, no," Eleanor said, holding up a hand. "You've nothing to apologize for. And really, the man is a bit of a scoundrel. You did well to put him in his place first thing."

Amelia half-grinned, half-grimaced. He'd hardly

been intimidated by her. He had been amused more than anything, drat the man. "I'm not sure I managed to put him in his place. I was the one with the pistol, but he seemed to be the one with the upper hand."

Eleanor fluttered her hand dismissively. "You know those military men—always acting as though they are in control of everything. I'm sure he was shaking in his boots underneath that bravado of his."

He was military, too? Amelia pictured him as he'd looked that morning. Immovable. Confident. Cocky, even. Bravado was exactly the right word. It made sense that he would be a military man. "If you say so. He is a friend of Mr. Norton's from the army, then?"

"He is. He and Nicolas served together for nearly two years."

"I wouldn't have guessed. He had such an unusual accent, I didn't think he was British." Yes, she was prying, but she was curious. Much more so than was usual for her. After Mama's death and all that followed, Amelia and her father both tended to steer clear of gossip.

But instead of answering her unspoken question, Eleanor's gaze slipped past Amelia's shoulder to the garden beyond the conservatory's wall of glass. "Speak of the devil! The men are back. Come, let's go greet them." She hooked arms with Amelia and grinned. "You and Lord Winters need a proper introduction, after all."

An unexpected surge of anticipation coursed through her as Eleanor hurried for the door, pulling Amelia along.

Proper? Nothing about the man had seemed proper this morning. Not his stubbled cheeks, not his sarcasm, and certainly not the way he had looked at her. The question was, would he be the same in the company of their friends? As odd as it sounded, she found herself hoping he would be.

She was sick to death of everyone always being so *nice* to her. Yes, they all meant well, with their pitying looks and gentle tones, but for once in her life, she wanted to talk to someone who didn't know about her parents. Someone who wouldn't tilt their head in that sad way, and whisper about "dear Sir Elroy and his poor daughter" as she walked by.

For once, she wanted to be around someone who was completely irreverent. Eleanor was great in the sense that she never treated Amelia with kid gloves, but she was a friend, and obviously there was kindness between them. Lord Winters was something else all together. He clearly had no reservations when it came to doling out sarcasm or challenging her.

She liked that. She didn't want that to change.

When Eleanor paused to open the door, Amelia put a staying hand to her arm. "Wait. Does Lord Winters know… That is, did you by chance tell him about—"

"No, of course not," Eleanor said quickly, shaking her head. "All he knows is that you are a neighbor. Well, that and that you aren't afraid to defend yourself." She gave her a playful nudge, and Amelia smiled in return.

Thank goodness. "All right. Thank you. It's not that I'd think you'd gossip, but…" she trailed off with a helpless shrug. "Let's just say people tend to think it's a detail others should know before meeting me."

Eleanor's smile dimmed just a bit, and she slid

her hand down to grasp Amelia's. "All anyone needs to know about you is that you are a kind, patient, beautiful woman with impressive aim."

Laughing out loud, Amelia nodded. "Yes, I think that last part is probably prudent." She tipped her chin toward the French door, through which she could see the men walking on the garden path toward the house. "Shall we?"

As they stepped outside into the sunshine, Amelia savored the silvery flash of anticipation that slipped through her belly. He might be impertinent, he might be vexing, and possibly even rude, but there was no denying that Amelia was rather looking forward to this *proper* introduction.

***

He hadn't expected to see her so soon.

But as he walked back from the stables with Norton, mud-stained and happy after an exhilarating ride, there she was. His own personal Venus, close at Miss Abbington's side as they walked out to greet them.

An unexpected jolt of pleasure went through him as Miss Watson's eyes darted up and met his. The contact lasted little more than a second before she directed her gaze to Norton. Gabriel took the opportunity to study her as the two greeted each other.

Even from ten feet away her eyes were startlingly blue against her rosy cheeks. She was tall for a woman, standing a good half-foot taller than her friend, and in this light, he could see that her thick, dark hair actually held hints of red. She could never fade into a crowd—not with such strong features. He liked that. He could never blend into a crowd either. In fact, he'd been told that his height and physique could be intimidating at first.

He pursed his lips. Perhaps he shouldn't judge her reaction this morning too harshly. He may be dressed as the gentleman he was, but it still must have been startling to happen upon someone like him on a deserted path. As a soldier, he had to appreciate the level of confidence she had exuded with that pistol of hers. It had never once waivered.

And regardless of what he thought of her or how she had treated him, she was a friend of his hosts and therefore must be treated with respect. Who knows, maybe she would turn out to be as pleasant as Miss Abbington.

Doubtful, but possible.

"I do hope you are enjoying this beautiful day," she said to Norton, her expression much more relaxed and welcoming than it had been for Gabriel.

Norton nodded. "Indeed we are. Nothing like a brisk ride through the English countryside to make the most of a fine afternoon."

Deciding it was best to just be his normal self and push past any awkwardness, Gabriel scoffed. "Brisk? Take another look at your dictionary, my friend. That ride could only be described as breakneck." He shook his head, chuckling lightly. "I can only assume you were in a hurry to return to the house. Imagine that," he said with a sly smile toward his friend, followed by a wink at Miss Abbington.

"No arguments there," Norton replied, sliding his arm around her waist. "And now I am doubly glad for it since our neighbor has come to call. Miss Watson, please allow me to introduce my friend, Lord Gabriel Winters."

Gabriel waited until her sapphire gaze met his before offering a challenging smile. "Oh, we've met," he said, his voice reflecting dark amusement as he dipped his head in an abbreviated bow.

"Actually, we haven't," she replied, quirking her brow with a touch of wry humor. "If we had been introduced properly, I doubt the morning would have progressed as it had."

His jaw tightened at her words. Of course it wouldn't have. With a proper introduction, she would have known of his station. In his experience, nothing turned an Englishwoman from sour to sweet quite like the words *my lord*. It had happened again and again since he'd inherited the title, and each time he became that much more cynical.

Whatever inclination he'd had to make a fresh start with her began to seep away. In its place, he reverted to the detached, devil-may-care attitude people expected of a young lord. "I'm perfectly content with how the morning progressed. If, however, you'd feel better if you apologized, I certainly won't stop you."

Her dark brows shot up like a pair of gulls taking flight. "Apologize? Whatever for? You were trespassing on our land. I believe my response was appropriate, given the situation." Ah, there was the glimpse of the woman he had met.

Norton cleared his throat, reminding them they had an audience. Biting back a smile, he addressed Miss Watson. "Knowing Winters, I'm certain you're in the right on this one. Although, now that you've been introduced, let's hope weapons are no longer necessary."

"We'll see about that," she murmured.

Gabriel stifled a snort. Whatever else he could say about her, she certainly had spirit. Was it possible that she wasn't as much of a lemming as he'd feared? He tilted his head to the side and smiled as his good humor resurfaced. "Come now, Miss Watson. Let us call a truce through the wedding, at the very least. I am to stand up with Norton, and I'd hate to be derelict on my duties."

"And after the wedding?" she asked, one delicate brow lifting in challenge.

He laughed and spread his arms. "After the wedding, you are free to take up arms against me at will." Yes, he was playing along with her, but damned if she didn't strike him as interesting. He liked it when she was a bit prickly. At least then, she didn't seem as though she were pandering to his bloody title.

Miss Abbington smiled and shook her head. "Careful, Lord Winters. I do feel it prudent to warn you that Amelia is quite a good shot."

Was she? He flicked his gaze in her direction. He'd assumed it had been for show. Not that he doubted she'd pull the trigger if threatened, but she didn't exactly look like an accomplished marksman. Perhaps it was the frilly dress and bonnet that had thrown him off. "Indeed?"

"Oh yes! She doesn't advertise the fact, but I have seen her practice before, and I daresay you wouldn't wish to be at the wrong end of her pistol."

Miss Watson's cheeks flushed with the compliment. "Thank you, Eleanor. You are much too kind."

Gabriel almost laughed. He could like a woman who preferred praise for her marksmanship over praise for, say, her looks or sewing skills. "Truly, the two of you are ruining all my preconceived notions of well-born British females." Notions he had come by the hard way.

When Miss Watson's brows lowered, he held up his hand. "That was a compliment, I assure you. With all the marriageable misses suddenly being thrust before me, I admit I had formed a rather unflattering opinion of your countrywomen."

What an understatement. Since inheriting the title four months ago, he had gone from invisible nobody to England's most eligible bachelor, just like that. During his first official season in the House of Lords, he couldn't walk out of his door without nearly tripping on some debutante or another being conveniently placed in his way.

As if he had any intention of taking an English wife. He knew exactly why everyone—particularly his father's family—was clamoring for him to find a woman of proper rank and lineage, and he'd be damned if he'd give them what they wanted.

Oblivious to his turn of thought, Miss Watson pursed her lips. "That was quite possibly the oddest compliment I have ever received. But I wonder, my lord, are not Englishwomen your countrywomen, as well?"

Norton snorted, shaking his head. "Oh, Miss Watson, you know not what you ask. Why don't the two of you take a turn about the garden so you can hear the whole, convoluted story."

Her blue eyes flicked to Gabriel, interest

sparkling in their depths. "I must admit, I'm properly intrigued."

"Excellent," Norton said, grinning broadly as he patted Miss Abbington's arm. "Shall we sit in the gazebo, Ellie?"

Gabriel nearly rolled his eyes. Obviously the man was just looking for an excuse to be alone with his bride. A tactic the lady in question seemed more than willing to endorse. "That sounds lovely. Do behave, Lord Winters. I can assure you my aunt is watching our every move from her sitting room."

Well, there was no getting out of it now. "Duly noted." Turing to Miss Watson, Gabriel offered his elbow. "Shall we?"

***

Amelia pressed her lips together as they walked, trying to hold her curiosity at bay. She didn't wish to seem too eager or gauche. He'd probably think she had some sort of *tendre* for him. He was definitely cocky enough to come to that conclusion.

After they had walked a few minutes in silence, she finally sighed and picked up the thread of their conversation. "Now that we've left the happy couple behind, I can stand the suspense no longer. Where, exactly, are you from, my lord?"

She glanced up at him just in time to catch him grimace. "Oh, I'm sorry. Is it a sore subject?"

"No, not at all. I'm still acclimating to the title and its address. As for your question," he said, looking out over the late-summer garden to the lake beyond, "that depends on whether we are speaking of the law or

23

the heart. By law, I am my father's son, born not forty miles from here in Kettering."

He said Kettering the way one might a curse word. Shaking his head, he glanced down at her, meeting her gaze. "But in my heart, I am the American my mother raised me to be."

There was defiance in his eyes, as though daring her to say something derogatory about his origins. Honestly, though, she had no idea what he meant. Choosing her words carefully, she said, "How exactly does one raise a person to be American?"

"By moving one to America, of course. My father died when I was only eight, and with no other ties or family in England—at least none that mattered—my mother went home." He shrugged, as though moving halfway across the world wasn't at all unusual.

"But I thought you and Mr. Norton were soldiers together. Did you return to serve in His Majesty's army?"

He gave a humorless chuckle. "Something like that. Now I find that I am curious, Miss Watson. How is it you came to be so handy with a pistol?"

It was a blatant change of subject, but if he wished not to talk of his past, then she, of all people, wouldn't press. "A girl living on a country estate with just her father and servants ought to be able to look after herself. It is simply the weapon at which I most excel."

The tension in his shoulders eased as he relaxed again. "Oh, so there were more weapons tried, then? The image of you with a pistol is hard enough to reconcile; I can't imagine what other deadly instruments I might have been confronted with."

"Daggers, swords, an ill-fated attempt at a sharpened hatpin. In the end, I found the pistol required the least amount of strength and agility."

As they walked, her fingers rested lightly on the creased fabric at the crook of his elbow. Every now and then his arm would move beneath her hand, and she could feel the bulge of his bicep against her the top of her thumb.

"Fascinating," he said, real interest infusing the word. "I never did have the patience for pistols. So much hassle in loading it, cleaning it, and keeping it handy. I prefer hand-to-hand combat."

"Well, of course *you* would." His size alone was probably enough to scare off most anyone.

He stopped, drawing back in surprise. "What is that supposed to mean?"

There was that defensiveness again. Smiling up at him, she said, "It means that you have brute strength on your side." As soon as the words were out, she wanted to take them back. For heaven's sake, she didn't want to sound like she was admiring his physique.

Which is clearly the impression he got. A wide, self-satisfied smile curled the corner of his lips as he crossed his arms over his chest. "Why, Miss Watson. If you are attempting to charm me, you are certainly succeeding." If he were a peacock, his whole plumage would be on display.

She rolled her eyes with great exaggeration, wanting to be absolutely certain he understood that she was in no way trying to charm him. "Merely stating the obvious. It certainly wasn't intended as a compliment."

His smile didn't dim in the least. "And yet,

that's exactly what it was. So, thank you. You flatter me." He winked and held out his elbow again.

Shaking her head, she took his arm, and they resumed the walk. The pebbles crunched beneath their feet, punctuating their companionable silence. It was odd, that it should be so easy to be with him. She hardly knew him, and yet they had the sort of teasing banter one might expect to have with a longtime friend. It was very unlike her.

And very nice.

After a few moments, he said, "Fighting isn't all about brute strength, you know. A smaller person can easily fell a larger opponent if he has an understanding of leverage. Or better yet, the element of surprise."

Her look was meant to convey just how plausible she found such an idea. "Right. The surprise I can believe, but I imagine the leverage only works to a certain point."

"You're wrong. Granted, a child probably couldn't defeat a full-grown man, but someone your size could certainly bring down a man of my size."

She snorted. "I'll stick with my pistols, thank you very much."

"You don't believe me?"

"Not particularly."

His free hand went to his heart. "You wound me, Miss Watson. Very well, you leave me no choice."

Knowing full well she was playing into his trap, she took the bait. "But to…?"

He smiled wolfishly. "Prove it."

She drew in a sharp breath, startled by the flutter of awareness that raced through her belly. No one talked to her like that. Ever since the tragedy of her mother's death, she'd been treated with kid gloves by anyone in the village, and Lord knew her father would never allow her to travel to Bath or London or anywhere else she might meet someone new. She swallowed, trying to gather her suddenly scattered wits.

His teasing, or flirting, or whatever they were doing wasn't going to lead to anything good. Amelia was painfully aware of the fact that she couldn't go acting as though she was interested in anyone, least of all a handsome, titled man with a devilish grin.

As casually as she could manage, she widened the distance between them. "On second thought, I suppose I should take your word for it. You are a former soldier, after all, so I'm certain you would know."

"Are you sure? It wouldn't be any trouble at all." The hint of cajoling in his voice only served to strengthen her resolve.

"Quite," she snapped, then immediately offered a smile to soften the word. She didn't want to come off as a shrew, but she needed some space. "I think perhaps we should head back to join the others."

His smile slipped and he slowed to a stop. "I apologize if I've made you uncomfortable. I was merely speaking in jest."

She should never have allowed herself to be caught up in their banter. Flirting and teasing with bachelors was reserved for blushing debutants and marriage-minded misses. She was neither. Her life was mapped out, and there was no point in tasting what could never be hers. Honestly, she should never have indulged her curiosity in the first place by coming here.

Home. She needed to return home to the life she knew and understood and felt safe in. Grasping onto the idea, she took another small step away from him. "Yes, I'm sure you were, but I still think it's best that we return."

His brown eyes reflected momentary confusion as his hands went to his hips. "Come now, Miss Watson," he said, his deep voice mildly reproachful. "I thought we had a truce. You of all people don't strike me as the sort to turn tail and run."

His teasing smile only served to make her more uncomfortable. Her stomach flipped, tempting her to give into to the easy intimacy of the moment. To forget all the reasons she needed to guard her heart every bit as vigilantly as she did her person. Purposefully, she pictured her father as he had been during his last fit. The panic in his eyes, the taut line of his shoulders and the white knuckles of his fists as he had clutched her hand.

Firming her resolve, she looked Lord Winters directly in the eye. "I don't know how they do things in America, but when a lady asks to be returned to her friends, a gentleman does so with out question."

***

Gabriel drew back at the look in her eyes, his good humor abruptly fleeing. What, was she suddenly offended by his company? Had his crude American manners scandalized her proper British sensibilities? God forbid he try to have a little playful conversation.

"Again, my apologies. I certainly don't wish to subject you to my ungentlemanly American self any longer than strictly necessary." He thrust out his elbow in order to escort her back, and she reluctantly accepted, her hand all but hovering over his sleeve.

"Thank you. I especially appreciate your being so *very* gracious about it."

He gritted his teeth. God, he hated that particular tone of condescension. The British were absolute masters of it. Miss Watson may be half a foot shorter than him, but she was somehow succeeding in looking down her nose at him.

"You know, it is little wonder you carry a pistol."

"Oh? Are you referring to the need to keep ill-mannered brutes at bay?" She gave him a false smile, surely knowing full well that she had called him a brute only minutes ago.

He shrugged. "That, and to protect yourself from the long list of adversaries you have undoubtedly collected thanks to your charming disposition."

Anger flashed in her eyes. "I assure you, Lord Winters. This 'charming disposition' is entirely unique to your presence."

"I suppose I should feel honored. Few men are privy to a woman's true nature."

She gasped, pulling her hand away from his arm. "Well, unfortunately, too many women are privy to men's true nature." There was a hitch in her voice that gave him pause, but before he could properly consider it, she straightened her shoulders and lifted her chin. "Now if you will excuse me, I will see myself home. Please convey my regrets to our hosts."

Turning on her heel, she headed back for the house, bypassing the path to the gazebo.

29

"Well, the two of you looked quite cozy walking in the garden today."

"Did we?" Gabriel hedged, offering Norton a bland smile. He wasn't feeling particularly chatty about how things had gone during that walk. He'd simply told them that Miss Watson had remembered a forgotten appointment, and hadn't wished to interrupt them.

In the hours since she'd left, he'd considered her sudden change in demeanor. One minute they were flirting, the next fighting. He had handled the whole thing rather abysmally, no matter how much she had insulted him. She was a friend of Miss Abbington's, and he should have just kept his damn mouth shut.

"You know very well you did, you old dog." Norton shook his head before taking a drink from his nearly full whiskey. "Why is it you have such a talent for attracting any unattached female within a five-mile radius of wherever you are? It's a talent I might be jealous of, if not for Eleanor."

Leaning back in his chair, Gabriel took a long draw from his cheroot. Blowing out a long breath, he said, "She was pleasant company." It wasn't a complete lie. He'd enjoyed the exchange up until she'd suddenly disengaged from him.

What was it with women in this country? They either clamored after his title or turned their noses up at his upbringing. Sometimes they did both. He suspected Miss Watson fell into that last category.

God, he couldn't wait until next spring, when he'd sail to New York to choose a wife. No one yet knew of his plans, but his father's family would absolutely choke on it when he came back with an American bride. As far as Gabriel was concerned, they—and the rest of the title-grasping *ton*—could go to the devil. After the way they'd treated him and his mother, he'd as soon wed Napoleon himself than marry an Englishwoman.

Norton cut his eyes over to Gabriel as he idly swirled his drink. "This one's not to be fooled with, my friend."

Oh for God's sake. "Please, I merely escorted her on a walk. I'm not going to go deflowering any virgins this trip." Least of all Miss Watson. He sighed. It was a damn shame things had turned out as they had. He wouldn't have minded having another person to talk to this week when Norton was otherwise occupied, and she'd shown promise for a while there.

"I'm just saying, she's more delicate than most. Eleanor told me a little about her past when you were walking, and well, just be careful."

Gabriel couldn't imagine anyone being less delicate. Amelia wasn't exactly a shrinking violet, especially when she had her pistol in hand. "If there was ever a female who could take care of herself, it's her. You do recall how we met, right?" He pointed his finger in Norton's direction, mimicking a pistol.

"Yes, well, there's a reason for that." He blew out a breath and set his drink down on the table beside his chair.

"Yes, I know. She's a shrew."

Norton's brows lowered, his disapproval clear. So much for Gabriel's attempt at being diplomatic. "That's not fair. She's a lovely women."

"Says the man who hasn't looked down the barrel of her gun." He flicked the ashes from his cheroot and took another pull. "Look, I'm sure she's a nice person, but she's one card shy of a full deck, if you know what I mean."

Shifting forward in his seat, Norton sighed. "I think there's something you should know about her. I don't want to be a gossip, but it's my understanding that this is common knowledge in the village. Apparently, her mother was killed by a pair of highwaymen when Miss Watson was only thirteen."

Gabriel blinked, momentarily shocked. "Holy hell." His gut clenched at the thought of something so violent befalling any woman. No wonder she carried a pistol. He grimaced, remembering how he had mocked her for it.

He thought of his own mother, who had died two years earlier from complications of a weak heart. He was still angry at the fact that she'd been taken too young, but at least it had been a natural death. The possibility of someone purposely cutting her life short was enough to make his blood run cold.

And he'd been a total arse to the girl.

He rubbed his eyes, hating the guilt that flared to life in his chest. He'd stupidly assumed her reaction to him had been about, well, *him*. He'd never imagined her defensiveness and standoffishness would come from a place of real fear or unease.

Norton set his drink down and crossed his arms. "After her mother's death, Sir Elroy became something of a recluse. In the early days, there were whispers that Miss Watson was more or less running the household.

Supposedly the baron has improved over time, but it's my impression that she's the one keeping things together."

Looking Gabriel in the eye, he said, "She's had more than her share to deal with in her life. Just try not to toy with her, all right?"

Gabriel nodded distractedly, pulling on his cheroot. He released a cloud of blue smoke and watched it rise toward the ceiling. How the hell was he going to make up for the way he treated her? Somehow, he doubted a simple apology would gloss over things.

He was a man of honor, damn it. He had to make some sort of amends. But how? What did he have to offer someone like her?

Nothing, really. To her, he was little more than a big brute of a man with boorish manners and—

Wait a second. That's exactly what he had to offer her. Earlier, she had laughed off his teasing suggestion that he teach her some fighting moves. But a woman who had been through what she had, and who had admitted to trying daggers, swords, and even a hatpin for possible ways to protect herself, could clearly benefit from the confidence one gains when one can defend oneself without the use of a weapon.

If his expertise could actually help her while assuaging his guilt for having treated her so poorly, wouldn't that be a win for both of them? Of course, after the way things had gone today, the real trick would be convincing her that he could help without getting himself shot in the process.

Chapter Three

*W*hat are you doing here?"

The breathlessness in Amelia's voice may have negated the stern tone she was going for. Lord Winters stood leaning against a tree at the exact place she had met him the day before, his arms crossed in front of him and a smirk already in place on his lips.

"And good morning to you, too," he said, as though they hadn't bickered like children yesterday.

Despite her determination to keep the encounter as impersonal and brief as possible, her heart gave a little flip at the sound of his voice. It was warm and slightly rough, as though he had just woken. His cheeks were smooth today, which was oddly disappointing. She drew a steadying breath. It didn't matter what he looked or sounded like—it was beyond improper for him to be here now.

Yesterday had been an accident. But this? And really, had there been any doubt of her intention not to speak with him again? Her hands found their way to her hips as she narrowed her eyes. "It can't be 'too' if I do not share in the sentiment. You are trespassing, as you well know."

He made no move to leave at all. If anything, he leaned toward her a bit. "I do know. And I was testing a theory. Apparently, the firearms only come out for strangers. Good to know."

She lifted a single brow. "I wouldn't count on that."

"I'm a soldier, Miss Watson, and a soldier always trusts his instincts." He took a step closer and angled his head to the left. "Would you like to know what my instincts are telling me?"

"If they are any good at all, they are telling you to leave. Now," she added, for good measure.

"Not at all," he said, his smile somehow innocent and devilish at once. "They're telling me that you'd like a lesson in how to defend yourself, in case you are ever caught without your trusty pistol. I'm certain you'd like as many ways to defend yourself against ill-mannered brutes as possible." He winked, as though sharing a joke with her. He was bantering with her again. It was as though yesterday's argument had never happened.

"It's a wonder you've survived this long if your instincts are as faulty as that." She lifted her head haughtily, determined to show him how foolish he'd been to come here this morning, and to prove that his dark, slightly disreputable good looks had no effect on her. "Now, if you'll excuse me," she said, preparing to sweep past him with all the regal bearing of a queen.

"See? My expertise could really help you. That

bordered on pathetic, as intimidation goes."

She glared at him. "I wasn't trying to intimidate; I was trying to dismiss."

"Either way, you failed dreadfully."

Shaking her head at his gall, she said, "Are you always this belligerent?"

He didn't even hesitate. "Absolutely. How else does one get what one wants in this world?"

It was like throwing pebbles at a brick wall. All her comments just seemed to bounce right off that magnificent ego of his. "What do I need to say to get you to leave, Lord Winters?"

"Nothing. I'm happy to leave—just as soon as our lesson is over."

"I feel compelled to remind you that though I may carry a pistol, I am very much a respectable woman. Receiving lessons from a bachelor alone in the woods is *not* acceptable."

He rolled his eyes, unimpressed by her remark. "It's not as though I'm going to ravish you, for God's sake. Don't think of me as a bachelor. Think of me as a tutor."

"I'm not hiring."

"Lucky for you, I'm volunteering."

Amelia let out a frustrated sigh. "You aren't leaving until you get your way, are you." It was a statement, not a question. She could see for herself that was exactly the case.

A single, decisive negative shake of his head was his only answer. And that ever-present smile, of course.

Annoyance tangled with a hint of anticipation.

She hadn't wanted him to come, and she knew very well he shouldn't be there, but there was something a little thrilling about standing in the woods together, completely alone. "Fine. Ten minutes, and then your 'lesson' is done and you go home."

Triumph lit his dark eyes as he nodded. "Agreed."

Shedding his jacket and draping it over the lowest tree branch, he paused to roll up his sleeves. Each turn of the fine lawn revealed another couple inches of his corded arms, his muscles moving this way and that beneath his pale skin. Her fingers itched with the desire to discover if his arms felt as strong as they looked. If the muscles were as taut, and the skin as smooth as she imagined. She curled her hand into a fist, trying to force away the completely unwelcome musings.

This was exactly why she had fled his company yesterday.

"Did I scandalize you just now?" His voice snapped her attention back to his face, which was all smug male amusement. He'd caught her watching him. "Offend those proper, well-bred sensibilities of yours?"

Of course he would catch her staring at him like some sort of milk-toast maiden fresh from the schoolroom. Making a show of rolling her eyes, she said, "No, you didn't scandalize me. I may be a female, but I'm hardly going to faint at the sight of a man's forearms." No matter how nice said forearms were.

"Really? What would cause you to faint, then? A bit of bicep, perhaps? A glimpse of chest?" He finished with his sleeves and settled his hands on his waist with a rakish half-smile. "Either of those can be arranged."

37

Oh heavens. She swallowed against the unwelcome flutter of nerves that thought elicited. Exasperated, she threw him an annoyed look. "And now you're just trying to shock me. I thought I was supposed to consider you a *tutor*." Still, she had to work to keep her eyes trained on his. His biceps? His *chest*? After glimpsing the splendor of his arms, she could only imagine what his chest would look like. The powerful build of a draft horse came to mind.

"Just a little harmless teasing. You English need to lighten up a bit. I'm sure in your circles, it's considered vulgar to even say the word *chest*."

"It's vulgar in most circles, my lord. I assure you."

"Oh? And I'm sure you're very worldly, tucked away in your idyllic little corner of England. You've seen what, three or four counties in your life?"

It was three, but she wasn't about to confirm it for him. She crossed her arms. "I may not be well traveled, but I can assure you, I am very well read."

He didn't quite roll his eyes, but it was close enough. "And do your gossip columns and novels give you vast insight into the human condition? That hardly compares with the knowledge one gains by actually experiencing a place. By interacting with people who are foreign to you and participating in cultures other than your own."

He couldn't know how desperately she wished to travel, how much she wished she could break free from the prison of Papa's anxiety and experience what the world had to offer. Even knowing all the terrible things that people did to each other, thanks to the grisly reports in the paper, even living with the consequences of her mother's attack, she still felt the heady pull of adventure thrumming in her veins. "You are determined to feel superior to me, aren't you? It doesn't matter that I read newspapers, *not* gossip columns, and am better versed in current events than most men. I don't branch out from my home county, and therefore, I'm fit to be mocked."

"Not mocked. Educated." He lifted his hands, palms out. "And you couldn't ask for a better teacher. I've had years of training in boxing, as well as some less civilized fighting. Should you ever decide to branch out from this little world of yours, I'll feel better knowing you can hold your own."

Out of nowhere, icy echoes of pain ghosted through her heart. Would things have been different if Mama had been taught to protect herself? Would she still be here today? Out of habit, Amelia's fingers slipped into her pocket and closed around the reassuring weight of the pistol's brass hilt. She was safe. She could take care of herself. And as much as she didn't want to admit it to him, these lessons might actually help.

Drawing a steadying breath, she nodded to Lord Winters. "Very well. Consider me your willing student."

***

It had been a gamble, coming here this morning. Gabriel couldn't know if she walked at the same time every day or even on the same route. And if, by chance, she did come by, he had no way of knowing if he'd actually be able to convince him to let her help. Particularly since she didn't know that he knew about her situation, and *especially* because of how they had parted yesterday.

But yet, somehow it had paid off.

She was right on all accounts: It was improper, imprudent, and certainly not the most intelligent thing for a man who wished to avoid the parson's noose at all costs. But she was remarkable, and damn it, he wanted to help her in some small way.

He smiled, genuinely this time, and nodded. "Excellent. Let us start with making a fist."

She scrunched up her nose as if he'd insulted her. "We needn't start as low as that. I know how to make a fist, thank you very much."

Smiling amicably, he said, "Mmhmm. Prove it."

Pursing her lips, she sighed and held up a clenched hand. Predictably, her thumb was tucked beneath her other fingers.

"You do not know how to make a fist; you know how to break a thumb."

"What?" She snatched her hand back, twisting her wrist in order to get a better look at it. "This is a fist, Lord Winters. Hand in ball. How else could you do it?"

"Relax your hand," he ordered, and she promptly followed his direction. He stepped forward and slipped his fingers around her wrist. Her skin was warm and wickedly soft against his. He heard her sharp intake of air but pretended he didn't. Otherwise, he'd have to release his hold, and he had no intention of doing that.

"'Hand in ball' is correct." He curled her fingers into her palm, then gently tucked her thumb into place. She gave no resistance, allowing him to guide her at will. Glancing to the fall of her dark eyelashes against her cheek as she looked down at their joined hands, he said, "You simply did the folding of fingers out of order."

He didn't move, even though his hand was still wrapped around her wrist. It was a light hold, the way one might idly curl one's fingers around the end of an armrest, yet he could feel the flutter of her heartbeat hammering away beneath his palm. Had she ever been touched like this? She was no young miss, yet tucked away in this tiny community, had she ever had a beau? Had she ever wanted one?

She glanced up to meet his gaze, her eyes the color of the ocean on the most brilliant of spring days. Good God—when had he ever made that kind of comparison before? He was here to help her, not admire her eyes. Swallowing, he drew back his hand, Norton's warning of last night flashing through his mind.

As if she were released from a spell, she blinked twice and looked back down. After a moment, she lifted her other hand and made another fist. "Better?" she asked, her voice slightly breathy.

He nodded. "Much." He stepped back, trying to remember why they had fought yesterday. Things really had been going well before she pushed him away.

She really was unlike anyone he had ever met. He liked the idea of pushing her boundaries a bit. There were so few women who walked the line between proper and scandalous as she did, without fully committing to one or the other. To him, such ladies were the most interesting.

"Right then. Hands up." He waited as she raised her properly formed fists. Compared to other females, her fingers were long and slender—just like the rest of her—but compared to the bear-paw hands of the men he was used to sparring with, her fists seemed delicate and absurdly feminine. The pretty blue-and-white gown didn't help things. His lips ticked up in a small grin.

"What?" she said, her eyes narrowing suspiciously.

"Nothing," he said, all innocence. He doubted if she would take it well if he told her how adorably ridiculous she looked just then. "Now, it's important to position yourself so that you can be as well protected from a blow as possible."

She promptly dropped her hands. "I'm going to get *hit*? Now, see, this is why I chose pistols. The person holding the gun will always have the upper hand."

He pursed his lips. She wasn't going to believe the importance of his lessons unless he proved it. "Take out your gun."

"Why?"

"Because I'm your tutor and I asked you to." He lifted an eyebrow, daring her to deny him. With an exaggerated sigh, she pulled the pistol from her skirts. He nodded his thanks. "All right, pretend I'm an attacker."

"As much as you exasperate me," she said dryly, "I'm not going to shoot you."

"Never say I didn't give you the chance." He offered a little wink, and she rolled her eyes as she lifted the weapon and pointed it at him, her finger well clear of the trigger.

"Very well. I'm ready."

Fast as lightning, he snatched the pistol from her hands and had it turned back around on her before she'd

42

even registered what had happened. Her eyes sprang wide open in shock. She looked first at him, then to her empty hands, then to him again. "How in the world did you do that?"

He handed it back to her, ignoring her question. "Again."

The wind ruffled the glossy mahogany curls surrounding her face, but she paid it no mind. Furrowing her brow, she palmed the grip, widened her stance, and aimed for his chest. "I'm not certain what sort of trick— hey!" Relieved of the weapon once more, she pressed her lips together and glared at him with reluctant admiration.

He grinned this time, passing the gun back and forth between his hands. "You were saying about having the upper hand?"

"Yes, fine. I do believe you have made your point."

A woman who could concede a point. He definitely liked that. "You, Miss Watson, are a very good sport."

"And you, Lord Winters, are a dreadful one." But there was a hint of amusement in her words. She held out her hand for the gun.

"Gabriel," he said on a whim.

Her eyes jerked up to meet his. "I beg your pardon?"

Now that it was spoken, he found that he liked the idea of her using his given name. They were in the middle of the forest. What would it hurt if they did away with the formalities? "Do me a favor and don't call me Lord Winters. The last three Lord Winters were real bast—er, unpleasant men." The understatement of a lifetime.

Her expression was dubious. "You can't be serious. I hardly know you."

"What does that have to do with anything? It's my name, just as yours is Amelia." He let the name slide over his tongue, enjoying the feel of it. "See? Neither one of us burst into flames for the use of it."

She shook her head, clearly unconvinced. "It's a sign of respect. I haven't given you permission to use my Christian name, so therefore you should not. Now, *Lord Winters*, give me my gun, please."

"Fine—I shall call you Miss Watson, and you shall address me as Gabriel, out of *respect* for my wishes. So, try again. Give me my gun…" He raised his eyebrows expectantly, waiting for her to finish the sentence.

Her lips pressed together in a mutinous line. Blowing out a breath, she said, "Give me my gun, Viscount Winters."

"Try again."

"Give me my gun, Major Winters?"

"No. And for the record, I was a lieutenant." With a sad shake of his head, he tucked the gun into the waist of his pants at the small of his back.

Her mouth dropped open. "What are you doing? Give me my gun, *good sir*."

"Do I look like a *good sir* to you?"

Her hands settled at her hips, pressing the fabric of her bodice tight across her chest. "No, not at the moment. Give me my gun, you knave."

"Knave? What, have we found ourselves back in

time? Shall I run and find a lance and codpiece? Wear a suit of armor and joust for the king's entertainment?"

There was a definite flicker of amusement beneath her stern expression. "Blackguard? Rake? Scoundrel? Let me know when I hit on the one that most closely describes you."

"You already know what will get me to relinquish my ransom."

"Ransom, indeed. You're being unreasonable."

"Now, now. I'm not an unreasonable man. You may get it back in one of two ways. Either ask for it *respectfully*"—he purposely teased her with the word—"or take it yourself." What was it about her that was so imminently teasable? Even knowing what he did of her past, it was so easy to volley with her like this. He liked to think it lightened that heaviness he kept glimpsing in her eyes.

Frustration crinkled her nose. "Neither of those are acceptable, as you well know."

He angled his head and put a hand to his ear. "I'm sorry, what was that? You don't wish to have it back?"

"Lord Winters—"

"Gabriel."

"*Gabriel*, give it back."

He wasn't prepared for the drop in his stomach the sound of his name on her lips caused. *Jesus.* After all that teasing he hadn't expected to be the one affected by their play. Forcing his lips into a smile and ignoring the sudden hammering of his heart, he pulled the pistol from his waistband and presented it to her. "Now, was that so hard?" His voice fell just shy of the glib tone he was aiming for.

"Yes," she said, giving him an arch look. She snatched the piece from his hands and shoved it into her skirt pocket. Stepping back, she folded her arms over her chest. "You do realize you will have to get used to people calling you Lord Winters?"

All too well. The last four months had been proof of that. "Unfortunately, yes. But it will take time for the words to represent something other than what they have in the past."

A soft breeze rattled the leaves around them, and she brushed an errant strand of hair from her eyes. "Were they really as bad as all that? The previous viscounts, I mean."

He gave a soft, humorless laugh. "And then some. My father and his sons from his first wife were cut from the same cloth. Large, overbearing men who liked to use their size and status to intimidate others."

She pursed her lips, her eyes sweeping up and down his frame. "Imagine that."

His jaw tightened. She was making the same comparison everyone always did. "Yes, I look like them, though with darker coloring. But I've never reveled in belittling those around me in order to feel superior."

"Of course not," she said quickly, shaking her head. "Forgive me, I was only teasing."

He raked a hand through his hair. "No, forgive me. If anyone has a right to point out my faults, it's you. And I apologize for that. You weren't wrong when you accused me of being an ill-mannered brute yesterday."

Her eyes softened as she offered a wry smile. "If you were a brute, then I was a shrew. I think it best we simply pretend the whole episode never happened."

Her words eased the guilt that had plagued him all night. Returning her smile, he said, "I think that is an excellent plan."

"Now see? Clearly you are your own man. Based on what you've told me, I very much doubt your father or brothers would have apologized."

He scoffed, nodding. "Suffice it to say, the three of them made my life hell growing up. An apology never once crossed their lips, even when Geoffrey broke my nose when I was seven. I was relieved beyond measure when my father died and we moved back to America." Why was he telling her this? He straightened, pushing aside the distaste the memories caused. "The positive side of it is that I learned from an early age the value of defending oneself, no matter one's size, which brings us back to our lessons."

Chapter Four

*A*melia hadn't expected to hit a nerve with the man. Clearly, there was a lot more to his past than she'd realized. There was no mistaking the pain that had flickered across his face as he spoke of his family. Her heart hurt for whatever torture they had put him through.

Despite her piqued curiosity, she didn't protest the change of subject or ask any more questions. Instead, she raised her fists to just below her chin. "Is this right?"

The wariness eased from his face as he inspected her position. "Not bad. Be sure to plant your feet shoulder width apart for better stability. Good. All right, let's see what you've got. Hit me."

Hit him? Her determination to follow his instructions faltered. "I can't hit you, for heaven's sake."

"What, are you afraid that you might hurt me?"

"No…"

"Then hit me. One shot, just to see your technique."

She let her arms drop a few inches and widened

her eyes at him. "I don't *have* a technique. And back up—I'll hit in your direction."

For a moment she feared he would push her, but instead he sighed and stepped back. "Your move, princess."

Narrowing her eyes, Amelia repositioned her hands and threw a delicate punch straight out. She felt more than a little ridiculous, but at least she'd done it.

His hands went to his hips, clearly unimpressed. "Where do you suppose is the strongest part of a man?"

Not a question she was expecting. Of their own volition, her eyes roamed his body and landed on the widest target. "His chest?"

"Exactly. So if you are aiming those dainty little fists of yours at a man, where do you suppose is the least effective place to hit him?"

She lifted her gaze to meet his. "His chest?"

He grinned. "Very good. I suggest aiming for the places that are most vulnerable. His stomach and ribs"—he moved a hand to the flat plane of his abdomen—"are good, but the jaw, nose, and temple are probably better, especially if it is unexpected. Try again."

Nodding, she swallowed and got back into position. She eyed his green-and-gold-striped waistcoat, trying to ignore the way it tapered toward his hips. Aiming for his lower ribs this time, she punched the air.

"Much better." Approval lightened his tone as he smiled. "Although, if you really want to cause some pain, you could aim a bit lower." Her cheeks flared with heat as she realized what he meant, but he kept right on with his instructions. "Make sure that when you punch, you don't think about stopping at your target."

He demonstrated, allowing his fist to stop short. "Instead, pretend you are punching right through it. That's when momentum will help." He struck out in a long, smooth arc, his hand nearly touching his opposite shoulder at the end of it. "Ready? This time, I want you to use my hand as a target, and be sure to follow through."

She, of all people, knew how to hit a target. Concentrating this time, she reared back before throwing all her weight into her punch. Triumph flared as her fist hit his palm with a resounding smack, but it was immediately doused when she stumbled forward. A squeak of alarm escaped her at the same time his fingers closed on her fist and his other hand darted to her waist to steady her. The heat of his hand instantly penetrated the light muslin of her morning dress.

"Steady there," he murmured, his words spoken startlingly close to her ear. "Are you all right?"

Sucking in a breath, she stepped back as soon as she had stabilized. "Yes. Thank you. My apologies." Once again, heat crept into her cheeks, and she looked down, studiously smoothing a hand over her skirts. Though he had released her, the warmth still lingered where his hands had been.

He shrugged. "No apologies necessary. You're an excellent student; it was my fault for not anticipating how much resistance I'd need to give you. Would you like to try again?"

"No," she said quickly, offering a sheepish smile. "I think I have the principle. Thank you for the lesso—"

He waved a hand, cutting her off. "No, I think you are right. I don't expect you to go around picking fights, so I don't imagine you'll need much practice in this position. It's probably more important to start with fending off advances. Grab my wrist, and I'll demonstrate how to break a hold."

He held out one hand, and she looked to it with a raised eyebrow. Grab his wrist? Staying here with him seemed less and less prudent as the morning progressed. Still, even as she knew she should leave, she didn't really want to. Not yet, anyway.

She'd never met anyone like him, and heaven knew she probably wouldn't again. The shock she had experienced yesterday had faded somewhat, and she wasn't so much afraid anymore as intrigued. He'd be gone soon, so why not be bold? Why not indulge that part of her that wanted a little adventure? Especially when he was teaching her valuable skills.

Taking a fortifying breath, she reached out and wrapped her fingers around his wrist. Just as when he had steadied her, her heart raced at the simple contact. For a moment he was still, and she wondered what he would do if she slipped her hand down a bit and laced her fingers with his. Lord, what an absurd thought. Just when she was about to lose her nerve and let go, he yanked his hands sharply downward, breaking her hold.

"Did you see how I did that?" He was all business now, his voice taking on the authority of a true instructor. Did he sense that she was doubting the wisdom of her decision to stay?

Copying his lead, she nodded briskly. "I think so."

51

"Good. Always tug toward the place where the opponent's fingers come together. If you try to pull toward his palm or back toward yourself, you'll just be wasting your energy. Also, be sure to turn your wrists so the little finger faces the direction you want to move your hand."

With no more warning, he grabbed her arm, imprisoning her wrist in a firm hold.

Her first instinct was to jerk backward, despite what he had just said. It was just so startling, having his hand on her so possessively. As he'd predicted, her move did nothing to dislodge his hold. Biting her lip, she tried again, this time following his instructions. When she was able to break free, Amelia grinned. "It worked!"

His stern expression of a moment ago vanished as he returned her smile with one of his own. "Imagine that. Perhaps you'll have a little faith in me now."

"Perhaps," she allowed, lifting her chin imperiously. It was rather empowering, successfully defeating someone of his size and strength. "Let's see if we can duplicate the results."

She held out her arms, holding her breath for the moment his skin would touch hers. He readily complied, closing his hands around both her wrists this time. A sparkling sensation raced through her and landed low in her belly, fizzing like soda water. Their position was no more intimate than dance partners preparing to waltz, yet her whole body hummed with his nearness.

Her gaze flickered up to his. His brown eyes were as rich and warm as strong coffee. He watched her, waiting for her to move. For the space of a second, she considered leaning into him. What would he do if she lifted her lips to his? What would it feel like to finally be kissed? Her heart pounded even harder at the thought. She *had* to get a hold of herself.

With a sharp jerk of both her arms, she freed herself from his hold. Heart still thundering, she took a step back and drew in a cleansing breath. The air around her was still flavored with his scent: the crisp smell of soap with warm hints of leather and spice.

This was dangerous. Not in the way she'd originally thought, when she first feared he might harm her, or even when she worried for her reputation. No, it was dangerous because every minute she spent with him, she seemed to find him that much more attractive. He made her feel stronger than she would have imagined she could without the benefit of her pistol. That was very heady indeed.

She was the one in danger of stepping outside her normal rules of behavior, and that was *not* acceptable. Rallying her wits, she said, "Well, I do believe our ten minutes are up. Thank you for the lesson."

Lord Winters's brows came together in surprise. It was abrupt, she knew, but she had to step away from the oddly charged atmosphere between them. He ran a hand through his dark hair, pushing it back from his forehead. "We've only just started. There is much more to learn, I assure you."

"Yes, I'm certain there is, but I must get back. My father worries if I'm late returning to the house." She smiled, ignoring the part of her that rebelled against leaving him. "I appreciate your time and talent, my lord."

He grimaced but didn't correct her. "It's my pleasure, Miss Watson. For tomorrow's lesson, I think perhaps we'll focus on more defensive moves like the wrist-hold break."

Tomorrow's lesson? A thrill raced through her, even as she shook her head. "Lord Winters—"

"Gabriel," he cut in, quirking a brow.

"*Lord Winters*," she said firmly, "it would be most imprudent for us to meet for another lesson."

"Yes, I agree." He slipped a hand beneath her palm and lifted it to his lips. He pressed a warm kiss to the back of her knuckles, shocking her with the feel of his lips against her bare skin. "Which is exactly why I shall be here."

She swallowed and tugged her hand back the moment he pulled away. "I'm sorry to say you will be wasting your time, as I shall not."

He shrugged and went to retrieve his jacket and gloves. "Your prerogative."

"I mean it. I won't come."

His smile was slow and entirely too confident. "Good day, Miss Watson. I'll see you in the morning."

Chapter Five

*S*eated on the chaise lounge in the library half an hour later, Amelia idly stared at the newspaper propped in front of her, even though she was hardly able to concentrate on contents after such an unexpected morning. She'd had to hurry to make it back on time, and her heart still pounded from the exertion.

Or perhaps it was the lingering effect of having Lord Winters's—Gabriel's—lips on her skin. While she was determined not to call him by his given name, she found that she kept thinking of him that way. *Gabriel.* How fitting. He may not act anything like an angel, but he was certainly as beautiful as one.

Another reason for her *not* to meet him tomorrow.

"There you are," Papa said, pulling her from her woolgathering. He made his way to his favorite chair and sat down before holding a note out to her. "We've had an invitation from Lady Margaret. She wishes for us to join her at dinner."

"How nice." Amelia smiled serenely despite the sudden surge of nerves that washed through her. She hadn't expected to see Gabriel again so soon—had been determined *not* to, in fact—but the prospect of doing so appealed to her immensely.

One look at her father's glum face told her he did not share her excitement. "So you say. I'd really rather not be out after dark. The roads…" He trailed off, shaking his head. "One never knows how safe they will be."

She stifled a sigh as she nodded. "Yes, I know. Although, did she say what time they are to dine? It may be that we could return before it's too late."

He glanced down at the paper, his eyes tracking back and forth over the words. "Hmm. Seven o'clock. We would arrive in daylight, but there is no way to leave in enough time."

The familiar flare of frustration made her teeth clench, but as always, Amelia took a deep breath and relaxed. "True. But it is only on the neighboring estate. And with Falks and the footmen with us, I'm sure it will be safe. Brackley has been very quiet of late."

But Papa was already shaking his head, worry creasing his forehead. "No, I still don't think it is wise. Perhaps we could invite them to dine with us tomorrow instead."

Patience is a virtue. She repeated the familiar phrase in her mind a few times. It wasn't Papa's fault that his nerves had been permanently overwrought since Mama's death. Amelia had repeated the saying when he insisted she chew each bite of food twenty times, just in case. She'd repeated it when he refused to allow her to go to London for her Season, and again when he'd insisted that she learn to swim fully clothed, on the off chance she ever fell in. And when she'd been forced to relinquish her candles at night so he could be sure she wouldn't accidentally fall asleep and somehow set the room ablaze with its unattended flame, her mantra was there.

She nodded as though in agreement, then paused, touching her finger to her chin. "Actually, I believe they are expecting a few more guests tomorrow. Miss Abbington's sister and Mr. Norton's step-brother will be arriving. And it truly would be a shame to turn down such a kind invitation."

He glanced back down at the missive, scrubbing a hand over his gray whiskers. "My, but this puts us in a bad position." Sighing, he shook his head. "Write a note back, would you, poppet? Send our heartfelt regrets, and let her know that we are very much looking forward to the wedding breakfast."

Dash it all! She really thought he might give in this time. Biting the inside of her cheek, Amelia nodded her assent. *Patience is a virtue.* Setting her paper aside, she rose and made her way to the escritoire. Fine, she would turn down Lady Margaret's invitation. She would forfeit a night in the company of friends. But tomorrow morning?

Suddenly she wasn't so sure.

***

Cool drizzle misted over Gabriel's face, its omnipresence making it impossible to avoid, even with his hat pulled low. Damn, he hadn't expected to be thwarted by the weather. Damp leaves rattled in the wind as though punctuating his thought. The rain wasn't so much falling as it was hanging suspended in the air, the superfine drops coating every surface. The path wasn't even muddy yet, though it probably would be within the hour.

Still, on the off chance that Amelia might actually show up, he wasn't going to give up yet. He rubbed a hand over his face, wiping away the moisture as best he could. He'd been disappointed to learn the baron had turned down the invitation to dine with them last night, but according to Miss Abbington, that wasn't uncommon. She hadn't come out and said anything against the man, but Gabriel gathered he wasn't the most reliable person in the world.

Well, Gabriel was nothing if not reliable. He planned to stay right where he was, planted beneath the sprawling oak tree they had practiced under the day before. The lessons had proven to be great entertainment, as had the woman. The more time he spent with her, the more time he wanted to spend with her. And what was wrong with that? A man enjoying the company of an interesting woman was the most natural thing in the world as far as he was concerned.

If only the woman would cooperate.

He turned and paced a few steps, willing her to be bold and come. When he turned to pace the other direction, it was as if he had summoned her from the mist. He stopped in his tracks, drawing in a breath at the sight of her. Swathed in a long hunter-green coat, she walked toward him with a confidence that lifted his heart. Her chin was held high, her gaze steady as she

58

returned his regard.

When she drew closer, he offered a pleased smile. "I approve of your prerogative."

Amelia chuckled, the corners of her eyes crinkling. "Well, with weather so fine as this, how could I miss my morning constitutional?"

He shook his head, unable to take his eyes from her. "Indeed," he agreed. Something about her seemed changed this morning. There was no hesitancy, no doubt in her choice to join him. Her blue eyes were brilliant despite the gray day, her glistening cheeks a becoming shade of pink beneath the fine sheen of rain. The drops clung to the curls framing her face and dampened the hem of her skirts.

She untied the ribbons of her bonnet and set it beside the oak's trunk. "Shall we pick up where we left off? I believe you mentioned other defensive moves like the one you showed me yesterday." She slipped out of her coat next, revealing a serviceable tan gown devoid of embellishment. Clearly she was here to work.

"Absolutely," he said, taking his own hat and laying it beside hers. He tugged off his gloves, then quickly shed his jacket, draping them both over the same branch he had used yesterday. He took her coat and laid it on his to protect it from the wet tree limb. "Would you like to start with what to do if someone tries to grab you from the front?"

At her nod, he stepped away from the tree trunk and motioned for her to join him on the path. "There are some places on the body that are more sensitive than others. If you've ever been pinched between the thumb and forefinger, you know what I mean. For today's lessons, we'll focus on using those points to our advantage."

He waited while she came to stand in front of him. Drops of water clung to her eyelashes as she regarded him expectantly. He still couldn't believe she had decided to join him in this weather. "As we discussed yesterday, the face is vulnerable. The jaw, the eyes, and the nose can all be exploited. But the ears are also every sensitive. If someone ever tries to grab you from the front, I want you to slap your palm as hard as you can against their ear."

Any other woman might be upset to be discussing such a dire topic, but Amelia seemed eager to learn. Not that he was surprised. Anyone who could brandish a pistol in a second flat wouldn't likely be bothered. In fact, her lips curved in a small grin. "Are you suggesting I box the person's ear like a wayward child?"

"Please don't tell me you had one of those awful militant governesses." Gabriel gave an overdramatic cringe.

"No, thank goodness. But I saw the vicar's wife keep her six boys in line with that technique a time or two."

"Yes, well, my oldest brother also liked to keep me in line with that technique. I can certainly attest to its effectiveness." It was a wonder he'd only suffered a damaged eardrum once. After that incident, his mother had been much more diligent in keeping the boys apart. When she could manage it, anyway. Gabriel's father disliked her interfering with the older boys' fun.

Setting aside the thought, he concentrated on the

topic at hand. "It's good that you know the basic concept. I'm going to come toward you, and I want you to go on the offensive. Don't wait until I reach you. As soon as I'm within range, swing at me with your flattened palm. Move as quickly as you can, like a snake striking its prey. Just do me a favor and don't actually follow through on this one." He gave her a lopsided grin. "I'd hate to hit the ground and muddy my clothes."

Doubt lifted her right brow. "I think you overestimate my strength."

"No, I think *you* are underestimating the technique. Ready?"

At her nod, he lunged toward her, arms outstretched as though to grab her shoulders. As soon as he was close enough, she swung her right arm up, stopping just shy of his left ear. The *whoosh* of air made him flinch involuntarily, and she smiled sympathetically.

"Memories of childhood?"

He grimaced. "No, just a natural reaction." And maybe a little memory, but she didn't need to know that.

"Are you saying I made you flinch?" Amusement flickered in her eyes.

Teasing, was she? He made a face. "As I said, a natural reaction. Just like this," he said, his arm darting out to within a few inches of her flushed cheek, making her blink. He smiled smugly. "See?"

"My father would call that having good reflexes," she replied archly.

He chuckled. "Yes, let's call it that. Now then, try it again, only this time I want you to aim just below the ear. There is an artery there that is another good target." He traced a finger down the side of his neck, demonstrating its location. "A good enough hit can really daze an opponent."

She touched a hand to her own neck, following the path he had shown. "I don't feel anything," she said, doubt clouding her words.

"It's there, I promise. And trust me—you don't *want* to feel anything."

They realigned themselves, and once again he lunged at her. She reacted at once, striking hard and fast with a flat palm. He immediately dropped to his knees, stunned by the hit.

Her eyes went wide with horror as she clapped both hands over her cheeks. "Oh my goodness! I'm sorry!"

Dampness seeped through the fabric at his knee as he stayed where he was a moment, gathering himself. "I'm fine," he said, giving his head a quick shake. She had one hell of a good aim that time. Pushing off the ground, he came back to his feet and rubbed his soiled hands down the side of his pants. He was already muddy, so it didn't matter.

She started to reach for him, then appeared to think better of it and instead crossed her arms tightly across her chest. "Are you certain? I'm so, so sorry. I had no idea it would work like that." Her misery was written all over her face. Gabriel found himself wanting to comfort *her*, despite the fact that he'd been the one knocked to his knees.

"Fine, fine. I assure you, I can handle a great deal more than slightly dampened breeches and a bit of dirt on my palms."

"I'm sure you are correct, but still." She shook

her head slowly, as though at a total loss. "I just can't believe I was able to do that. You're as big as an ox."

His eyes widened. As big as an *ox*? After a moment's deliberation, he decided to take it as a compliment. Swallowing a grin, he said, "That was perfect. You did just as you should have, and I am perfectly fine."

His words might have been feathers for all the impact they had on her. She pursed her lips. "Do you know, I think I am properly prepared for the world now. Thank you for the lessons." Nodding once, she started to march past him.

Oh no, he wasn't letting her go that easily. Reaching out, he snagged her by the elbow. "Don't be ridiculous. There are many more ways to bring a man to his knees yet to be learned."

She didn't resist his hold, even though she now knew how, thanks to yesterday's lesson. Good—he had her attention. Instead of meeting his eyes, her gaze settled on what was sure to be a red spot at the side of his neck. Raising her free hand, she gingerly touched it. "Do you think there will be a bruise?"

The touch surprised him. Her fingers were light and soothing, but still his pulse kicked up. Swallowing, he released her wrist and stepped back from her touch. "I doubt it. Now, we are moving on to the next lesson."

She shook her head. "No, we are not. I won't be responsible for injuring you further."

"If we don't go on, my pride will be injured beyond repair."

"Better your pride than your person."

He rolled his eyes. "I promise we can go slow,

so there is no danger of any injury." For whatever reason, he didn't want to let her get away just yet. If she was willing to come in the rain to meet him, then he was willing to do whatever it took to keep her there. "We can even reverse roles, if it makes you feel better. Though, I do think it would look a little silly for little you to try to attack me."

"Little me?" She scoffed, clearly offended. "I'm taller than most any other woman I know."

"So does that mean you'd rather reverse roles, or shall we just continue at a slower speed?"

Sighing hardily, she finally acquiesced. "Yes, fine, we'll go in slow motion."

He did his best to keep his triumphant grin to a minimum. Before she could change her mind, he nodded his approval. "Excellent choice. For this move, I'm going to grab your shoulders. Like the last one, the key is not to fight strength with strength. When your life depends on it, you fight dirty.

"What I want you to do is deliver an open-palmed slap to both my eyes like this." He tapped his face to demonstrate. "Understood?"

"Yes, I think so."

He reach out and laid his hands on either side of her neck. His palms grazed the delicate swoop of her collarbone, and his thumbs brushed the bare skin at the base of her neck. He drew a slow breath through his nose, trying to ignore the feel of her damp, silky skin beneath the roughened pads of his fingertips. "Whenever you're ready. And go as slowly as you like," he added, his voice slightly gruff.

She raised her hands on cue and gave a light tap

to both his eye sockets. Her hands were exceedingly gentle this time, so much so that she barely touched him.

He released his hold on her shoulders and lightly gripped her wrists. "You're a little high," he said as he guided her hands into place. "You want your fingers to connect with the eyelids while the palm slaps the cheeks."

Her fingers were cool against his face, and he lowered her hands without thinking and rubbed them between his own to warm them. Her eyes widened, the bottomless pits of her pupils seeming large enough to get lost in.

"Do you want to try again?"

Amelia shook her head slowly. "No, I think that's good."

Reluctantly, he released his hold on her hands. Each time they touched, it seemed a little harder to let go. "I think one more should be good for now. I'd hate for you to catch your death out here with me."

A smile lifted the corner of her beautiful mouth. "I think you'll find I'm made of sterner stuff than that."

He readily returned her grin. "I think you are right." He wanted for her to stay the whole day with him, but he knew that wasn't possible. Even he realized that would be pushing the limits too far. Clearing his throat, he said, "Is there any situation you would like to know how to escape?"

Tilting her head, she thought for a moment. "What about if someone grabs me from behind?"

He nodded and made a little twirling motion with his finger. This attack seemed the most impossible to get out of, but there was one guaranteed way to get a man to release you. The difficulty was how to put it in a way that wouldn't completely scandalize her.

She obediently turned around, presenting him with her back. Amelia's dark hair was piled high on her head, and it was impossible not to admire the slender length of her neck. Gabriel stepped right up behind her, sternly admonishing himself to stay on task. The light, floral scent of her hair wasn't helping things. She smelled like summer rain, and it was all he could do not to slide his hands around her waist and draw her closer to him.

"All right. I'm going to wrap my arms around you, and I want you to pay attention to what you can and can't do in that position. Are you ready?"

"I am."

Taking a deep breath, he settled his arms around her. It was far and away the most scandalous thing he had ever done with a proper young woman. He closed his eyes for a moment, refusing to give in to the desire to transition into an embrace. Swallowing, he said, "Now is your chance to see what you can move."

He realized almost at once his mistake when she started to wiggle against him. Her hips slid back and forth as she tried to extract her arms. She went on for a few moments, shimmying this way and that. He gritted his teeth, forcing himself to stay detached.

Finally giving up, she shook her head. "I'd say I'm well and truly trapped."

"Not at all," he replied, keeping his voice low since his mouth was so close to her ear. "You can move your hips, can't you? And your lower arms?"

She nodded, turning her head to look at him.

"Yes, but I can't seem to do anything of use."

Her breath, sweet and warm, fanned across his cheek as she spoke. God, this was as close to a lover's embrace as one could get. His heart kicked in his chest, and he pressed his eyes closed, trying to keep his wits about him. These lessons were the best and worst idea he had ever had.

After a few seconds, she shifted in his arms. "Lord Winters," she murmured.

"One second," he said, trying to overcome the thrum of his blood in his ears and right the tilting sensation in his gut.

Cold hands touched his forearms as she relaxed back against his chest. "Gabriel."

The sound of his name on her lips was like setting a match to tinder, undoing all his efforts. He opened his eyes, tilting his head in order to look down at her. Her gaze was settled squarely on his lips, her own mouth slightly open as her chest rose and fell with each rapid breath.

For a moment, neither of them moved. They were suspended in time, a hairbreadth away from giving in to the desire that stretched between them like an electrical current. She opened her mouth, and he knew that her next words would send them both over the precipice. The only thing he wasn't sure of was whether they would fall backward or forward.

Chapter Six

*A*melia had no idea what had changed between them. One moment, they were deep in their lessons, and the next her heart was thundering, her whole body crying out for the feel of his lips to hers. All the longing she'd ever felt in her life seemed to come roaring back all at once, overwhelming her with the desire to finally be kissed.

And not just kissed—kissed by him. *Gabriel.*

The man who saw *her*, not the tragedies of her past. The man who teased her and bantered and made her heart pound. It was something she had sought to avoid, but now that the moment was here, she was helpless to deny the powerful pull of attraction. Lifting her gaze to his, she whispered, "*Please.*"

She didn't have to say it twice. Instantly, his mouth was on hers as he tightened his arms around her. Sparks showered through her belly like fireworks cascading through the night air. Enveloped in his warmth, cradled in his embrace, she relinquished all control, letting him lead her. It was her first kiss, and she shouldn't have had the first clue what she was doing, but it felt so perfect, so incredibly natural, all the nervousness she might have had fell away completely.

His lips parted, and the tip of his tongue traced the seam of her lips. She hesitated, not sure what to do, not even sure what to feel. He started to pull away, as though her hesitation was a sign that she didn't want more, so she twisted in his arms, turning so that she could wrap her arms around him, too.

He paused, as if unsure whether to go on, but a moment later he slid his arms more fully around her waist and deepened the kiss. This time, when his tongue touched her lips she readily opened to him. Her stomach danced as their tongues twined. He tasted of lemon and honey, tart with a hint of sweetness, and so perfect she never wanted the kiss to end.

The rain started to pick up, but she barely noticed. Water trickled down her face and onto her chest, cooling her heated skin. After a time—a few seconds? A minute? It was impossible to tell—Gabriel slowed the kiss, pressing his lips against hers once, twice, three times before finally pulling away.

Neither one of them spoke at first. She looked up into those gorgeous, velvety-brown eyes, wondering where on earth her sanity had gone and why she didn't care.

Smiling, he slid a knuckle beneath her chin and guided her lips to his for one last kiss. "That," he said, his voice low and raspy, "was not the lesson I had in mind."

A grin came to her lips. Lord have mercy, she'd

just kissed a man. All these years she'd been so sick of being protected, of being held back and coddled, she'd probably been hoping for just this exact outcome without even realizing it. "I hope you can forgive me for taking advantage of you like that."

He barked with laughter. "I believe that is supposed to be my line." He shook his head. "I think I've just made a complete mess of the student-tutor relationship."

That was an understatement. They'd both crossed a line that couldn't be uncrossed. Lord knew there was no way she could convince herself she was only here for the lessons now. Still, she found she couldn't regret it. She *wouldn't* regret it. She may have done little more than torture herself with a taste of something she could never have, but right then, with her lips still damp and her heart still fluttering, it seemed worth it. "Oh, I don't know. I definitely learned a lot just now."

The comment didn't have the effect she expected. Instead, his eyes grew serious, and he scrubbed a hand over his face, swiping at the moisture that dripped down his forehead from his hair. "That really shouldn't have happened. You're a respectable woman and I'm...me."

She tilted her head. "What is that supposed to mean?"

Wariness dulled his eyes as he gave a little shrug. "I mean, it was wrong for me to kiss you, seeing how there is no understanding between us, nor could there be."

No understanding? For heaven's sake, it wasn't

as though she was expecting an offer of marriage. In fact, she didn't *want* one, and couldn't accept even if he offered one. Her father's state would never allow for her to marry and move away. Still, it stung that he felt he needed to lay out the fact that there was to be nothing between them. "My, aren't you a romantic. Just what every girl wishes to hear upon her first kiss."

He raked a hand through his hair, slicking it back from his face. Cursing under his breath, he said, "I'm mucking things up, and that is not my intention. You are a lovely woman, Amelia. You don't need a scoundrel like me messing things up in your life."

All the warmth of moments ago seemed to dissipate all at once, and she wrapped her arms around herself. "Oh, for the love of Pete. It's not as though I am going to trap you into marriage based on one kiss. And you are right about one thing: I don't need a man like you, anyway."

Her pride stung painfully, all the more potent with her mortification. She turned and marched to where her bonnet lay, every step feeling awkward. Cramming it on her head, she yanked the ribbons into a knot, all the while glaring at the viscount. "If you'll excuse me," she said, brushing past him.

"Miss Watson, wait."

Miss Watson? Amelia only moments ago and now she was Miss Watson again? She paused, lifting a single eyebrow in question.

His hands dropped to his side as though unsure of what to say now that he had her attention. He shook his head. "I'm sorry."

"As am I, Lord Winters." With that, she hurried

71

back toward the house, feeling like the worst sort of fool.

***

Gabriel was not looking forward to the wedding.

Which made him feel even more like a bastard than he already did. Here he was, supposed to serve as witness on the most important day of his friend's life, and all Gabriel could think about was what a royal arse he had been the last time he'd seen Amelia.

What the hell was wrong with him? How on earth had he managed to take advantage of the very woman he had been trying to help? Her first kiss should have been reserved for her future husband, not some wretch just passing through. Especially knowing how sheltered she'd been most of her life.

Sighing, he inspected himself in the mirror one more time. His cravat was neatly tied, jacket brushed and perfectly in place. His boots reflected the morning light filtering into his bedchamber. Fleetingly, he mourned the loss of his regimentals. The navy jacket he wore made him look far too much like the viscount he now was.

Three sharp taps sounded on the door. He turned and called over his shoulder, "Enter."

Norton let himself in, his whole face lit with the most jovial of smiles. "Winters, my good man. The time is at hand. Tell me, how do I look?" He spread his hands wide, inviting inspection. He wore his dress uniform, looking as sharp as Gabriel had ever seen him. Happiness came off him in waves, his whole body radiating a sort of anxious energy.

Keeping a straight face, Gabriel said. "Jesus, man, could you at least smile? You look like you're going to a funeral."

Norton laughed out loud and clapped a hand to Gabriel's back. "Didn't you know? I am. Time to bury the bachelor life for good."

Pushing aside the dread that lined his stomach like lead at the thought of seeing Amelia again, Gabriel returned his friend's grin. "I've never seen a man so happy to rush into the parson's noose. Far be it from me to keep you waiting. Shall we?"

Less than an hour later, they stood together in the village's small church as Miss Abbington held Norton's hand, repeating the vows that would tie them together forever. Her eyes sparkled with tears of joy as she spoke, even as her cheeks must have ached from the smile that wreathed her face.

Norton said his vows next, his voice strong and confident, easily carrying over the small congregation. Miss Libby Abbington sniffled from the first pew, her arm tightly entwined with her aunt's. Lady Margaret wiped away a tear with her free hand, her face absolutely glowing with pride.

Gabriel let his gaze slip over the congregation, knowing exactly who he was looking for. He found her toward the back, seated beside a gray-haired man with wide mutton whiskers. Amelia's eyes were trained squarely on the happy couple, and Gabriel allowed his gaze to settle on her for a moment. She looked beautiful in her cerulean gown, a color that, even from this distance, made her eyes stand out. Her mahogany hair was arranged in neat curls, so different from the way she had looked the last time he had seen her, when they had both been soaked.

He dropped his eyes to his hands, picturing her as she had looked that day, a study in contrasts. Strong but vulnerable. Innocent but world-weary. Proud but wounded.

Wounded by him.

Damn it all. He had to talk to her at the wedding breakfast. He had to try to make things right after making such a royal muck of it all.

The vicar was wrapping up the ceremony, and Gabriel turned his attention back to his friends. As the groom slipped the ring onto his new wife's finger and stole a kiss before God and man, the congregation erupted in an impromptu little cheer.

Gabriel smiled, happy for Norton and his blushing bride. It was so nice to see love triumph in the world they lived in. His gaze flicked back to Amelia, whose eyes were still trained on the bride and groom. She was smiling, though it didn't seem to reach her eyes.

He clenched his jaw, determination stiffening his spine. Come hell or high water, by the end of the day, he *would* make things right for her.

***

As the carriage rumbled toward Lady Margaret's house for the wedding breakfast, nervous energy gathered in Amelia's belly. It had been so hard not to look at Gabriel in the church, especially when she could feel his eyes on her. She'd gritted her teeth, absolutely determined not to meet his gaze. It had been two days, and lingering embarrassment still heated her cheeks.

"Are you feeling quite all right, poppet? If you're unwell, we should return home immediately."

It was tempting to say yes, knowing she would be whisked back home and likely never see the viscount again. But Eleanor was her friend, and she wanted to celebrate with her. Besides that, she was no coward. She wasn't about to run away just because she felt like a fool. Pressing her lips into a smile, she shook her head. "I'm perfectly fine, Papa."

Uncertainty hovered in his eyes for a few seconds, but finally he nodded and settled back against the squabs. She turned her attention to the window, watching the familiar trees lining the road to Lady Margaret's home pass by.

It had made her heart swell, seeing the happiness in her friend's face. Witnessing the look in Mr. Norton's eyes when he gazed at his bride had been wonderful and awful all at once. Wonderful to know Eleanor was so thoroughly loved, terrible to realize that no one would ever look at her like that.

And even if they did, what then? She couldn't leave her father, not with his nerves. Yes, she longed to travel, to see all the places she read about. Yes, even as she still suffered from the mortification of her first kiss, she nonetheless wanted to share such an experience again someday. She had come alive in a way she had never known during that kiss. For the first time in her life, no thoughts or worries had clouded her brain. She had been free to do nothing but *feel*.

If only Gabriel had left it at that.

No, he had to go ruin the whole thing. His sudden worry that she might somehow force him to marry her based on single kiss still stung her pride. She was not some sort of desperate woman, eager to lay claim on the first man who looked her way.

She sighed and rubbed a hand over her eyes. So much for adventure.

Half an hour later, the celebration was in full swing, with a veritable feast spread out and a string quartet providing lively music on the terrace. Three dozen or so guests milled about, laughing and talking as they admired the food, the clothes, and the exceedingly happy couple.

Amelia stood by the stone balustrade overlooking the garden, sipping a glass of lemonade and watching several of the village children dance around the garden in time with the merry music. Out of the corner of her eye, she saw a large, dark figure approach, and she gripped her glass with sudden nerves. *Gabriel.*

"Good morning," he said simply, stopping a respectable distance away. "You look beautiful in that color." His voice was low and respectful, all too formal compared to what she was used to from him. Not that she was surprised—he wouldn't want her to get the wrong idea about his intentions.

Unable to delay it any longer, she met his gaze and nodded. "Lord Winters."

Pressing his lips in a straight line, he nodded. "It seems as though I have earned that title, for once."

She blinked, tilting her head in question. What was that supposed to mean?

"As I said before, the past Lord Winters have all been, well, less than gentlemanly." He gave a small shrug. "It seems that I am to join their ranks."

From what little he'd revealed about his family, she knew what an insult it was for him to say such a

SCANDALIZED BY A SCOUNDREL

thing. Sighing, she said, "You're not as bad as that. You merely made some rather…unflattering assumptions."

"Let us say it like it is. I acted like an ass, and you're quite justified in being angry at me." That was the tone she recognized. Slightly acerbic, vaguely self-deprecating—but thankfully, no longer painfully polite.

"I'm embarrassed, not angry at you. Regardless, it doesn't matter. You'll be leaving shortly anyway." For some reason, that thought caused a sharp pang of regret. No matter how it had ended the other day, he was the most exciting thing that had happened in her life in a very long time, and he would soon be gone.

He watched her for a moment, his dark gaze seeming to go right through her to her innermost thoughts. "Care to take a walk with me?" He held out his arm, tempting her to take it.

After a brief hesitation, she nodded and slipped her fingers onto his elbow. The faint scent of leather and spice teased her senses, reminding her of being wrapped so fully in his arms, enveloped by his warmth.

They stepped down the stone steps into the garden and set off on the outermost path, away from where the other guests had congregated.

"My father's family is quite beside themselves, you know."

She furrowed her brow and glanced over to him. This was not the direction she had anticipated their conversation would go. "I beg your pardon?"

"My uncle and his progeny," he clarified, his eyes trained on the white pebble path in front of them. "They condoned my father's second marriage because they so desperately needed the money. And because my

77

father had already produced two sons of proper lineage. They didn't like it, but viewed it as a necessary evil."

She had no idea what to say to such a thing, so she simply let him continue. Admittedly, she was curious to know more about him.

"They never had anything to do with my mother and me, neither before nor after his death. We were inferior in every way as far as they were concerned. Most especially my mother, despite the fact she had saved them all."

Gravel crunched beneath their feet as they walked, the strains of the quartet growing fainter with each step. Why was he telling her this? It did seem rather personal. Still, her heart ached for the repressed pain she heard behind his matter-of-fact tone. "That's terrible. No one should be made to feel that way, especially not by one's family."

He nodded, looking out over the lake. "And now the upstart they never wanted to acknowledge is the head of the family. Ironic, no?" Shaking his head, he said, "If they could, they'd happily see me dead so my uncle could reclaim the title for the untainted line of the family."

She hadn't realized how bad things were for him. "If you hate the title so much, and the family wants it so badly, why don't you abdicate and be free of it?"

A muscle in his cheek hardened as he clenched his jaw. "My mother gave up everything to abide by her father's wishes and marry a nobleman. It was her money that saved the estate from ruin, yet the very moment my father died, she was tossed aside like some common beggar. Thanks to the marriage contract, she did receive her widow's portion, but the majority of the money stayed with the estate."

Amelia pursed her lips, considering what he'd said. "So you want what is rightfully yours." It wasn't unreasonable, given how terrible his family sounded.

He stopped, turning to face her fully. The determination tightening his features was so intense she almost took a step back. "I don't give a damn about the money or the estate. But over my dead body—literally—will I allow the family to have it. In fact, it's my intention to return to America next month to find a bride. If a half-American viscount sends them into hysterics, I can't wait to see what a three-quarters American will do to them."

The bitterness of his words was shocking, even as it was understandable. "I…see." Sort of. It was hard to fathom that kind of situation.

He raked a hand through his hair and blew out a long breath. "What I am trying to say is that I have a plan, and I shouldn't have allowed myself to get carried away. It wasn't fair to either one of us. All I was trying to do was help you, and I ended up hurting you instead."

Now she saw why he was sharing this. "Really, it is all right. I never…" She trailed off, blinking as she realized what he had just said. "Wait, *help me*? What do you mean by that? The lessons were all in good fun."

His eyes shuttered, and he nodded. "Yes, of course."

Suspicion wended its way through her wary heart. "Gabriel, why would you need to help me? Did someone tell you that I needed help?"

"No," he said quickly. After a beat of silence, he

added, "But after learning why you carry your pistol, I thought perhaps it would help your peace of mind to have other self-preservation techniques to fall back on."

Dash it all. Someone had gossiped. All this time, she had thought him free of the pity that seemed to follow her like the plague. She believed he was interested in her, spending time with her because he wanted to, not because he pitied her or thought her in need of his charity.

Fresh mortification welled up inside her. Had he kissed her out of pity, too? She had begged him, hadn't she? She had as good as asked to be kissed, he had complied and then worried that it might somehow interfere with his plans. She took a step back, putting distance between them.

"Ah, yes. Everyone is always so kind when they hear of my family's misfortune. The poor baroness, who had resisted the loss of her mother's necklace and had, ultimately, lost it and her life with the flick of a dagger. The poor baron, who was never the same after his wife's death, always terrified his only daughter would be taken from him, as well. And the poor girl, who not only grew up motherless but half raised herself thanks to the baron's weakened mind.

"The same girl who taught herself to shoot better than any sharpshooter the army ever produced, just so her father would see she would be safe. The same girl who was cosseted anyway, kept carefully tucked away from the dangers the outside world offered. The same girl who has been pitied by everyone who knew the story, and thought, just once, there was a person out there with whom she might have a clean slate. Someone who would treat her like a normal person, and maybe, just maybe, liked spending time with her."

Tears pricked the back of her eyes, but she forcefully blinked them away. Gabriel looked stricken, completely taken aback by her unexpected rant. And it *was* unexpected. She could hardly believe she had spoken so plainly. Drawing herself up to her full height, she said, "Well, thank you very much for your charity. Consider my mind at peace. If I can return the favor someday, do be sure to let me know."

Sucking in a fortifying lungful of the rose-scented air, she turned on her heel and stalked back to the house. This time he didn't call after her or try to stop her.

Chapter Seven

*T*he scratch at her door came hours later, when it was almost five o'clock. The butler opened the door and bowed. "Pardon me, Miss Watson, but you have a visitor: a Miss Abbington. Are you at home?"

Amelia's brows came together. Definitely not who she would have expected—not that she was expecting anyone. Gabriel was probably halfway back to Kettering by now. Laying her book down on the sofa cushion beside her, she nodded. "Yes, of course. Please see her in at once."

A few moments later, Preston escorted a young, pretty blond woman with wide brown eyes and an irrepressible smile into the room. "Miss Elizabeth Abbington."

As the butler withdrew, Amelia stood and came forward to greet the girl. "Ah, Eleanor's sister. I'm so sorry we didn't have the opportunity to meet today. I must ask, is everything all right?"

"Oh yes. Please don't fret. You left your wrap

behind, and I thought it the perfect opportunity to meet you. I hope you don't mind," she said, presenting the wrap in question.

"No, of course not." Amelia accepted the cream-colored shawl and gestured to the sitting area situated before the fireplace. "Please, let us sit down and have a chat." She paused to ring for tea before settling back into her spot on the sofa.

"A chat sounds wonderful. Aunt Margaret has taken to her room to rest following the day's festivities, and my cousin Will has gone off to the pub with Lord Winters."

Gabriel was still here then. Amelia grabbed onto this little tidbit, tucking it away like a useless treasure. "How did you find the celebrations today? It was so wonderful to see the newlyweds so happy."

Miss Abbington nodded, her cheeks dimpling. "Oh yes. Wasn't it though? I'm so glad Aunt Margaret could sneak me away from Hollingsworth for the joyful occasion. My uncle will probably disown me if he discovers I came, but I'm not altogether convinced that would be a bad thing."

Amelia wasn't about to comment on that particular topic, though Eleanor had shared a bit about her manipulative uncle. "Will you be in town for long?"

"Only for a week, then I have to get back. But with Eleanor and Nick off to Brighton tomorrow, I hope you don't mind if I make a pest of myself coming to visit. Elle has spoken quite well of you, and I do so love making new friends."

"I would be honored to have you here." And she meant it. Eleanor's sister may be young, but Amelia could already tell she was easy to talk to.

"Are we friends then?" At Amelia's nod, the girl grinned. "Excellent. Then I insist you call me Libby, and I hope you don't mind if I call you Amelia as my sister does."

It was impossible not to like the girl. She somehow managed to be wonderfully sweet and terribly forward all at once. "By all means, please do."

She leaned forward in her chair, rubbing her hands together. "I'm so glad, because now that we are friends, I can get to the real reason why I came here."

Her *real* reason? Amelia almost didn't want to ask. "And what reason is that?"

"You must forgive me, for I am a terrible busybody." She held her hands up as if staving off judgment. "Rest assured, however, because I only wish to *know* things—never to gossip about them. You can ask Eleanor. I will take my treasure trove of knowledge to my grave."

What on earth was one to say to something like that? Luckily, the tea arrived then, giving Amelia a moment to gather her thoughts as she poured them each a cup. Keeping her eyes trained on the steaming spout as she poured the hot water, she said, "I'm not at all certain I can add to that treasure trove of knowledge."

Accepting her teacup, Libby smiled with confidence. "Let us find out, shall we? I'll start with an admission of my own: During the ceremony, I spent very little time watching Nick and Eleanor. I was much more interested in watching the tall, dark, and handsome Lord Winters."

Amelia was suddenly very glad her own teacup

was still on the tray. Glancing up warily, she waited for Libby to continue. The girl was watching her right back, her eyes wide with interest as though gauging her reaction. Finally, Amelia said, "Well, you are free to observe whomever you choose."

"Indeed. And that observation was made all the more easy since the good viscount's attention was wholly focused elsewhere."

Taking a careful sip of tea, she did her best not to reveal that she already knew that. The weight of his gaze had nearly been a physical force. "Yes, I suppose that does make it easier."

Libby nodded amicably and tipped her cup to her lips. Swallowing, she said, "It was what I observed that had me anxious to speak to you. Tell me, Amelia, are you aware that he is in love with you?"

Amelia glanced up sharply, nearly dropping her cup. "He is most certainly *not* in love with me. We barely know each other." Still, her silly heart pounded fiercely in her chest at the suggestion.

"Well, he quite fooled me. The way he looked at you..." She sighed, shaking her head. "Let us just say that someday I very much hope to be on the receiving end of a look like that."

Unexpected heat tinged Amelia's cheeks. Why on earth would Gabriel be looking at her like that? He clearly wanted little to do with her. Any interest he had in her was motivated by his feeling sorry for her. Wasn't it? Her stomach fluttered as she recalled his heavy-lidded gaze just before he had kissed her. His lips had been seeking, eager against hers. Yes, she'd asked him to kiss her, but hadn't he pulled her flush against him?

Had not his arms encircled her waist as though he never wanted to let go?

"I would pay any sum to know what you are thinking about right now."

Dash it, these thoughts would get her nowhere. Amelia tried not to look guilty as she met Libby's very interested gaze. "I was merely wondering what had caused such an odd look from the viscount. I suppose I could remind him of someone."

"Mmm," Libby murmured, nodding in agreement. "Of course, you two did look rather cozy when you walked off together during the breakfast." She raised her brows, clearly expecting some sort of response. When none came, she shrugged good-naturedly. "Very well, I won't pry. Just know that if you do decide you wish to talk with someone, I'll be here. Or rather, I'll be at Aunt Margaret's.

"Now then," she said, setting down her cup and leaning over the armrest of her chair. "What is it you do to fill your days out here in the country?"

Half an hour later, Amelia waved goodbye to her new friend. It had been a very pleasant visit, but it had been impossible to stop thinking about what Libby had said about Gabriel. Had he really watched her in the way Libby described? Amelia knew that it certainly wasn't love, but it very well may have been a reflection of genuine interest.

She thought about her earlier reaction to his disclosure that he knew of her family's past. He really had seemed stricken. Had she wrongly accused him? Yes, her situation may have motivated him to offer the lessons, but was that such a terrible thing? In all the time they had spent together, she never had sensed any pity in his interactions with her.

Worrying her bottom lip, she paced the length of the drawing room. It was obvious there could never be anything between them. Not with his plans, and certainly not with her father. But she had come to care for him, and he'd given her that incredible first kiss. It pained her to think of him leaving at all, but most especially with them permanently parting on such poor terms. He had been kind to her—teasing and irreverent and even charming, in his own way—and she had thought the very worst of him.

She had no way of knowing when he was leaving. He could be gone at first light, for all she knew. What she did know was where he was right then: the village pub. She glanced outside. The sun was just touching the tops of the trees, still nearly an hour away from setting.

Nibbling her thumbnail, she considered her options. She could wait until tomorrow and visit the neighboring estate, risking missing him if he left early. She could let it go and never make amends for the way they had parted. That one she immediately discarded. The very thought of never hearing from him again was enough to make her chest hurt. Well, then, she could write him a letter, apologize for her overreaction, and wish him well in his life.

Or…

Or she could seize the opportunity for a little adventure. The village was only two miles away. What if she went there now and intercepted him when he left the pub? She knew what his horse looked like, so it wouldn't be difficult. Yes, darkness would fall before she could return, but it wasn't as though they were in London.

Her father would be overwrought if he knew what she was considering, but after the activity that morning, he had retired to his bedchamber an hour ago. She'd never defied his wishes before, but what he didn't know surely couldn't hurt him. She didn't waste another moment considering the prudency of what she wanted to do. Coming to her feet, she bypassed her newly returned off-white wrap and hurried to her room to grab her dark cloak and change her shoes.

She was going to town.

***

Gabriel had no idea why he had agreed to accompany Norton's stepbrother to the village. At the time, a stiff drink or two had sounded like a good idea. Yet, after an hour nursing his whiskey and watching Ashby have a bloody good time with the locals—many of whom he'd known from previous visits—Gabriel was beginning to wonder what the hell he was doing here.

He thought it would be a good way to take his mind off Amelia and how her shoulders had looked as she'd walked away. He'd been stunned by her outburst, but after she was gone, he'd realized how all of it must have looked to her. He hated that she'd been hurt, hated that he had no way to fix it, but there was nothing he could really do about it, other than to leave as quickly as possible so she could go about the business of forgetting he ever existed.

He doubted he'd ever be able to do the same.

She was a true original. In a matter of days, she'd somehow started to matter to him. He didn't even give a damn that she was English. He cared about her, whether she believed it or not, and he could already tell he was going to miss her like hell.

And right then, all he wanted to do was leave this place and brood in peace.

As if reading his mind, Ashby broke away from the men he was talking to and threaded his way through the throng to Gabriel's table. "Not quite sure this is your crowd, Winters. I've found my way home alone plenty of times, and I can do it again tonight if you prefer to head back." He grinned distractedly as a busty barmaid called out, "When are ye going to buy me a drink, Wills?" and gave her assets a good shake.

The man's offer was tempting, but Gabriel shook his head. "I don't want to abandon you."

"Nonsense. I may very well abandon *you* if you stay." He waggled his eyebrows at the pretty barmaid, earning a saucy wink in return.

Gabriel chuckled, fleetingly glad that the affable young heir seemed to be the polar opposite of his father. If even half of what Norton said about the Earl of Malcolm was true, it was a wonder Ashby had turned out so well. Setting down his whiskey on the scarred wood table, Gabriel nodded. "Very well. If you don't mind, I think I'll do just that. I want to get an early start tomorrow, anyway."

Ashby grinned, offered a loose salute, and headed toward the waiting maid. Tossing a few coins on the table, Gabriel stood and quickly made for the exit.

The cool evening air was the perfect antidote to

the stuffy, overheated pub. Closing his eyes, he tipped his head back and drew in a long breath, grateful to have escaped.

"Gabriel."

His eyes flew open at the sound of her voice. *Amelia.* He turned and spotted her just around the side of the building. She wore a long, gray jacket with the hood lightly perched at the top of her head. Why in hell would she have come here, of all places?

He hurried over, ignoring the surge of pleasure he felt at the mere sight of her. "What are you doing here? Is everything all right?" He followed her a few steps around the corner into the wide alley, where they were out of direct view of the street.

Her blue eyes were luminous in the waning light, and he couldn't seem to look away. God, she was so beautiful. The urge to touch her, to slide his fingers down her pale cheek or run his hands through the dark silk of her hair was almost overwhelming, but he resisted. He didn't want to upset her, not after the way they had parted.

"Everything is fine. I just…" She paused, licking her lips before starting again. "I just had to see you before you left. To apologize."

She had come to find him here, all alone, so she could apologize? To *him*? "If anyone should apologize, it's me. I mishandled everything, from start to finish."

"No, you didn't," she insisted, shaking her head. She looked up at him with those soulful, sapphire eyes and said, "I overreacted. Badly. I understand why you were concerned that I might misunderstand your intentions and why it was so important to you that I

90

knew where things stood. I imposed my own insecurities on the situation, and that wasn't fair. You did not deserve my anger."

"Amelia," he breathed, wishing like hell he could pull her into his arms and comfort her. "Please don't. You did nothing wrong. Your reaction was honest, and you shouldn't ever apologize for that."

Her lips curl into a tiny, regretful smile. "I've spent my whole life cooped up and protected, and you gave me a taste of the adventure I've been longing for. Thank you." She lifted onto her toes and pressed a soft, sweet kiss to his cheek.

He closed his eyes as his heart thundered in his chest. Her scent was like a drug, daring him to give in to the desire that flooded his whole body. When he opened his eyes, he could see exactly how close she was. So near that if he only turned his head an inch or two, her lips could be his.

He swallowed, willing himself not to move. She started to lower back down from her tiptoes, but she stilled halfway and raised her gaze to his. Indecision warred on her lovely face, even as her breathing increased.

"Gabriel," she whispered, leaning into him.

He fisted his hands at his side, determined to let her have complete control. He swallowed thickly. "Yes?"

"If I promise that it won't mean anything, will you kiss me goodbye?"

If it didn't mean anything? At this point, such an idea seemed impossible. Looking toward the street, he slipped his hand behind her back and tugged her farther

into the alley, where the chance of anyone seeing them diminished. Dusk was beginning to fall, casting them in shadow and giving the illusion of privacy. He licked his lips and gently wrapped his arms around her. Pressing his forehead to hers, he said, "Are you certain?"
She nodded, the movement small but impossible to misinterpret. In that moment, she was his. Something inside him broke loose at the thought, and without waiting another second, he lifted his hands to her jaw, cupping her face as though she were made of the finest porcelain. Slowly, purposefully, he lowered his lips to hers.

Chapter Eight

A thousand butterflies took flight in her belly as
Gabriel's mouth pressed against hers. Amelia groaned
with the pleasure of the moment, memorizing the way
his body felt against hers and the scent of leather and
spice that would forever remind her of his kiss.

She didn't even realize they were moving until
her back touched the cold stone of the wall behind her.
She lifted her chin, opening fully to him, accepting the
exquisite glide of his whiskey-flavored tongue as it
danced with hers. God, but she'd been right to come.
This was the goodbye they were meant to have. This kiss
did justice to the intensity of their short time together.
He may have only stayed for a week, but she'd
remember it, and most especially this kiss, for as long as
she lived.

Too late, she heard the footsteps behind him.
She broke the kiss, but before she could so much as
blink, a meaty fist slammed into Gabriel's temple, the
sound of flesh against bone sending terror racing down
her spine.

His eyes rolled back in his head as he collapsed

ERIN KNIGHTLEY

to the ground like a sack of flour. It all happened so fast. Amelia started to scream, her hand fumbling for her gun, but in an instant the man was on her, his fingers closing roughly around her throat, cutting off her scream along with her air supply. Dimly, she realized there were two of them, her attacker and another man standing over Gabriel, emptying his pockets with one hand while holding a broad-bladed knife in the other.

Panic flashed through her, more vivid than anything she had ever experienced. White spots popped into her vision as she struggled to pull the man's hands from her throat to no avail. He was leaning into her, pressing her hard against the wall as his hands maintained their steely grip. The more she fought, the more he squeezed.

God, she was going to die.

Just like her mother, just as her father had always feared—she was going to die at the hands of a filthy criminal. *No,* she wouldn't allow it to happen. She'd trained to protect herself, hadn't she? She tried to break through the panic, push past the dizzying haze that clouded her air-starved brain. What was she supposed to do when someone held her like this? *What?*

All at once, Gabriel's calm, authoritative voice flashed though her mind. *You want your fingers to connect with the eyelids while the palm slaps the cheeks.*

With the edges of her vision growing dim, she scrambled to rip off her gloves. Once free, she raised her bare hands and slapped against the man's eyes with every bit of strength she possessed in the world.

His head snapped back as he let out a shocked cry. His backward momentum dislodged his hands from her throat, and she clambered to get away even as she gasped desperately for air. The other man cursed and jumped out of the way, stumbling over Gabriel's prone form in his haste.

She didn't have time to recover—she had to move *now*. With her blood hammering wildly through her veins, she jammed her hand into her pocket, closed her fingers over the familiar brass grip of her pistol, and yanked it free of her skirts. The man with the knife recovered his balanced and charged at her, his blade extended menacingly in front of him.

Amelia swung the gun up in a smooth arc, bringing him to an abrupt halt. He exchanged glances with his partner, clearly unsure of what to do. Widening her stance, she moved her arm back and forth, pointing the pistol alternatively between the two men. "Get back," she growled, her voice raspy but fierce. Surprise registered on both their faces, but they didn't retreat.

The taller man, the one who had tried to choke her, narrowed his eyes as his lip curled into a sneer. "Ye can't shoot us both. Ye can bet the other will be on ye the second yer shot is spent."

She straightened to her full height, glaring at them with all the ferocity of a woman who had spent her whole life fighting against the fear of just this sort of thing. They would *not* win. "You're right. I cannot shoot you both. But I *will* shoot one of you. And I promise you, I will make that shot count."

They hesitated, exchanging another glance. She could almost hear them debating her competency, woman that she was.

She took advantage of their indecision, lowering

her aim. She may have been sheltered, but even she knew what part mattered most to a man. "Which of you would like to go to your grave missing a very important part of your anatomy?"

That got their attention. The confident smirks slipped as both of them covered the area in question with their hands. It was then that Gabriel stirred, groaning as he struggled to sit up. Relief course through her with an almost dizzying intensity. He was all right, thank God.

He blinked, confusion creasing his brow as he tried to focus. Suddenly his eyes widened, and he was up like a shot. Without a second's hesitation, he lashed out at the closer of the two men, kicking his leg out from under him at the same time he drove an elbow in the man's face. Gabriel moved like lightning, already attacking the second man before the first even hit the ground.

In a matter of seconds, both men were unconscious on the ground and the knife was safely tucked in Gabriel's boot. She gaped at him, her eyes rounded with shock. She'd never seen anyone move as fast or as effectively in her life, especially for a man of his size. He hadn't been lying when he said hand-to-hand combat was his area of expertise.

His gaze flickered back to her, roaming from the top of her head to her feet and back. "Are you injured?" Desperation clouded his words as he panted for breath, though he didn't move from his position over the two unconscious men. "Please tell me you are all right."

She lowered her weapon and nodded, trying to breath past the relief that clogged her throat and weakened her limbs. "Mostly intact. Nothing compared to the injury you sustained." Already his right eye was swelling, and a thin line of blood trickled from the corner of his brow.

Despite the seriousness of the moment, despite the two men crumpled at his feet and the fact he was still breathing hard, he smiled. "My hero. It appears you were right after all." He gestured limply to her gun. "He who has the pistol has the upper hand."

She shook her head, tears unaccountably blearing her vision now, when she was safe. "No. I never would have gotten away without your lessons. He tried to choke me, so I slapped his eyes."

All humor abruptly vanished from his eyes. "He laid his hands on you?" When she nodded, his nostrils flared. "Which one?"

She pointed to the closer of the two. Turning, he delivered a sharp kick into the blackguard's ribs. Blowing out a breath, he straightened and looked back at her. "You should go."

She blinked. After all that, he was telling her to leave? "What? Why?"

"I need to deliver these men to the authorities, and I'm assuming you don't want anyone to know you were here."

He was right. If her father found out, he might never recover from the shock of it, or from his disappointment in her. As it was, she suspected she would have to be creative with her clothes for the next few days to hide the bruising at her neck. Nodding, she slipped her pistol back into her pocket. "Will I see you again?" Her throat tightened as she said the words. The thought that she might not left her breathless.

He bobbed his head once. "Tomorrow morning?"

No, that wasn't good enough. She couldn't possibly wait that long. She shook her head.

"Tonight, then."

Swallowing, she nodded. "I'll be waiting."

***

It was a good hour before Gabriel was able to get the two bounders sorted out. Apparently, they'd heard about the wedding and thought to capitalize on out-of-town revelers. As Gabriel suspected, neither had been inclined to say a word about the woman who had overcome them.

Now, as Gabriel approached the old oak they had met at before, he could barely breathe with the need to see Amelia again. He needed to touch her, to see with his own eyes that she was truly all right. She was there, waiting in the darkness for him.

He dismounted his horse and tossed the reins over a low-hanging branch, not even pausing in his need to feel her in his arms again. She didn't wait for him to reach her. Striding forward, she met him halfway, neither of them stopping until their arms were wrapped tightly around each other. He held her securely in his arms, squeezing his eyes shut as he rocked from side to side.

When he could finally draw a proper breath again, he loosened his hold and stepped back, inspecting her face in the moonlight. "Are you certain you are well? I think I lost ten years off my life when I came to and realized what was happening."

She nodded, taking a long breath before

exhaling. "Yes. I'm shaken, but I'll be fine. Thanks to you." She slipped her hand around his and gave a little squeeze.

He laced their fingers together and brought her knuckles to his lips. After brushing a kiss to each one, he said, "My apologies for being so distracted that I didn't hear their approach. As for the lessons, I did nothing but teach you a few tricks. You were the one who saved yourself. Both of us, in fact. I've never met a braver, stronger, more amazing woman in my whole life. And now that I've found you..." He paused, giving a helpless shrug. "I find I don't want to let you go."

She stilled, her eyes looking deeply into his, searching. "What are you saying, Gabriel?"

Was that hope in her voice, or was he hearing what he wanted to hear? He shook his head, hardly able to believe that she had so thoroughly turned his life upside down in a matter of days. "I'm saying that I don't want to give you up. I'm saying that I'm not going to let my hatred of my father's family prevent me from being happy. I'm saying that maybe"—he tugged her a little closer—"I should forgo my trip to America next month and come here instead."

She closed her eyes, blowing out a breath before gazing back up at him. "But my father..."

Smiling, he purposely flexed his muscles, letting her feel his strength. "Your father may like the idea of his daughter marrying an overlarge brute of a former army officer with a talent for incapacitating would-be criminals. Did not I just hand over two lowlifes to the magistrate?"

Worry knitted her brow. "But you don't know

him like I do. He won't be able to just let go of the anxiety that plagues him."

"Amelia, I have all the time in the world. I'm confident I can win his affections. But answer me this: Have I won yours?" He waited, heart pounding, for her answer. He had every confidence that, with time, he could convince her father that he would protect her. But that didn't matter if the woman herself didn't share his conviction.

Her grin was the most wonderful sight he had ever seen. Nodding, she said, "Indeed. Though for the life of me, I don't know how. Eleanor warned me you were a scoundrel, you know." Her eyes glimmered with mirth, and he chuckled in response.

He exhaled a breath he hadn't even realized he'd been holding. "Well, thank God you didn't listen to her. After all, I find I'm in need of a bodyguard, and I doubt I could do better than a woman of your considerable talents."

She laughed, the joy of the sound washing over him. He kissed her then, long and hard. He was very, very much looking forward to sparring with his sweet Amelia for a long time to come.

Epilogue

"*Y*ou look just like your mother, poppet."

Amelia met her father's gaze in the mirror as he came up behind her and settled his hands on her shoulders. Tears sprang to her eyes at the peace she saw in his expression. She pressed a hand over his. "I do?"

He nodded, a soft smile touching his lips. "You do. She wore a gown just that shade of blue on our wedding day, as well." Slipping his hands from her shoulders, he reached into his pocket and produced a small strand of pearls. He carefully placed it around her neck and fastened it into place. "Which is why I thought the necklace she wore that day would look just right."

"Oh, Papa," Amelia said, turning and burrowing her face into his chest. The tears slipped down her cheeks, dampening the crisp, white fabric of his cravat. "Thank you so much. They're beautiful."

It had taken over six months for Gabriel to win her father over. He had been patient and kind and full of a quiet confidence that had eased Papa little by little. It helped, of course, that Gabriel was as brawny as Falks, as skilled a fighter as any professional boxer, and as protective as a bear of its cubs. Her father seemed to recognize that Amelia would be safer with Gabriel than just about anyone else on the planet.

Papa still had his days, but for the first time since her mother's death, he seemed to find some measure of peace. "Yes, well, promise me that you will take care of them. And yourself," he added, a hint of worry clouding his eyes.

She smiled, reassuring him with a nod. "You know I will." She didn't tell him that she had her pistol tucked into her pocket even now. Today, it wasn't for fear or protection. Today, it was her "something old." Her good-luck charm, really. Her stomach fluttered just thinking of the day she and Gabriel had met and the role it had played in their unusual courtship.

Kissing his cheek, she said, "And you can come visit as often as you like, of course. Just as we will visit here frequently." It had been particularly helpful that Gabriel's home was only half a day's carriage ride away. The same home that would be hers after today.

The ride to the church was quiet as she held her father's hand and stared out at the land she had called home for her whole life. It had been her sanctuary and her prison, shielding her from not only the bad, but also from all of the good life had to offer. She could hardly believe that all the things she once had never dared to even dream about were now becoming her new reality.

The carriage slowed to the stop and her heart flipped with the sudden rush of excitement. Her father disembarked first then turned to help hand her down. As she emerged into the bright spring sunshine, she glanced around at the pretty flowers lining the path leading to the church's entrance. There she spotted Gabriel, tall and so very handsome, standing with his hand arrested on the knob, his eyes riveted on her.

When their eyes met, he broke into the brightest, widest smile she'd ever seen and gave her a little wave. Unexpected tears blurred her vision as she grinned and waved back. Her pulse surged with anticipation. In a few short minutes, Gabriel would finally be hers!

Her father chuckled and gently wrapped her hand around his elbow. "Are you ready?"

A wave of happiness washed through her, filled with optimism, love, and hope. The sorrow and darkness were truly behind them, and the future ahead was very bright, indeed. Grinning broadly, she nodded. "More so than I've ever been in my life."

No more fear. No more holding back. Her adventure, her *life*, was about to begin.

About the Author

Despite being an avid reader and closet writer her whole life, Erin Knightley decided to pursue a sensible career in science. It was only after earning her B.S. and working in the field for years that she realized doing the sensible thing wasn't any fun at all. Following her dreams, Erin left her practical side behind and now spends her days writing. Together with her tall, dark, and handsome husband and their three spoiled mutts, she is living her own Happily Ever After in North Carolina.

Find her at www.ErinKnightley.com, on Twitter.com/ErinKnightley, or at facebook.com/ErinKnightley

Made in the USA
Coppell, TX
30 June 2020

29797639R00066